A WITCH'S TOUCH

A SEVEN KINGDOMS TALE 3

S.E. SMITH

MONTANA
PUBLISHING

ACKNOWLEDGMENTS

I would like to thank my husband Steve for believing in me and being proud enough of me to give me the courage to follow my dream. I would also like to give a special thank you to my sister and best friend, Linda, who not only encouraged me to write, but who also read the manuscript. Also to my other friends who believe in me: Julie, Jackie, Christel, Sally, Jolanda, Lisa, Laurelle, Debbie, and Narelle. The girls that keep me going!

And a special thanks to Paul Heitsch, David Brenin, Samantha Cook, Suzanne Elise Freeman, and PJ Ochlan—the awesome voices behind my audiobooks!

—S.E. Smith

A Witch's Touch: A Seven Kingdoms Tale 3

First E-Book Published January 2018
Cover Design by Melody Simmons

Summary: A young witch is saved by a police detective who is searching for two missing women, and she discovers he may be able to help her save her people.

ISBN 9781985582019 (KDP paperback)
ISBN 9781078746908 (BN paperback)
ISBN 978-1-944125-23-3 (eBook)

Romance (love, explicit sexual content) | Action/Adventure | Fantasy (Urban) | Fantasy Dragons & Mythical Creatures | Contemporary | Paranormal

Published by Montana Publishing, LLC
& SE Smith of Florida Inc. www.sesmithfl.com

CONTENTS

WHO'S WHO IN THE SEVEN KINGDOMS

The Seven Kingdoms:

Isle of the Elementals – created first

King Ruger and Queen Adrina

• Can control earth, wind, fire, water, and sky. Their power diminishes slightly when they are off their isle.

• Goddess' Gift: The Gem of Power.

Isle of the Dragons – created second

King Drago

• Controls the dragons.

• Goddess' Gift: Dragon's Heart.

Isle of the Sea Serpent – created third

King Orion

• Can control the Oceans and Sea Creatures.

• Goddess' Gift: Eyes of the Sea Serpent.

Isle of Magic – created fourth

King Oray and Queen Magika

• Their magic is extremely powerful but diminishes slightly when they are off their island.

• Goddess' Gift: The Orb of Eternal Light.

Isle of the Monsters – created fifth for those too dangerous or rare to stay on the other Isles

Empress Nali can see the future.

• Goddess' Gift: The Goddess' Mirror.

Isle of the Giants – created sixth

King Koorgan

• Giants can grow to massive sizes when threatened – but only if they are off their isle.
• Goddess' Gift: The Tree of Life.

Isle of the Pirates – created last for outcasts from the other Isles
The Pirate King Ashure Waves, Keeper of Lost Souls
• Collectors of all things fine. Fierce and smart, pirates roam the Isles trading, bargaining, and occasionally helping themselves to items of interest.
• Goddess' Gift: The Cauldron of Spirits.

Characters:
Magna: half witch/half sea people. She is Orion's distant cousin on his father's side
Drago: King of the Dragons.
Carly Tate: Banking Associate from Yachats, Oregon
Drago Jr. (DJ): Drago and Carly's oldest son 4 years old
Stone: Drago and Carly's second son 3 years old
Jenny 'Roo': Drago and Carly's daughter 2 years old
Orion: King of the Sea People
Jenny Ackerly: School Teacher and Carly's best friend
Dolph: Orion's 8 year-old son from his first marriage
Juno: Orion's 5 year-old son from his first marriage
Kapian: Orion's Captain of the Guard and best friend
Kelia: Orion's elderly nursemaid
Kell: Magna's father
Seline: Magna's mother
Ashure Waves: King of the Pirates
Bleu LaBluff: Ashure's Second-in-Command
Nali: Empress of the Monsters
Ross Galloway: Fisherman from Yachats, Oregon
Mike Hallbrook: Detective for Yachats, Oregon Police Department
Ruth Hallbrook: Accountant and sister of Mike
Koorgan: King of the Giants
Marina: Witch
Isha: Captain of the Guard for the King and Queen of the Isle of Magic;

Marina's older brother.
Magika: Queen of the Isle of Magic
Oray: King of the Isle of Magic
Geoff: Marina's younger brother
Erin: Marina's younger sister

SYNOPSIS

As the darkness spreads, help comes when she needs it the most…

Marina Fae never considered herself a powerful witch or dreamed that she could make a difference in the fight to save her people, but when the Sea Witch's magic swept across the Isle of Magic, Marina led a group of children to safety in the dense mountain forest, and it was the only the beginning of what she discovered she can do.

Detective Mike Hallbrook has been searching for two women who disappeared in Yachats State Park. There is something truly odd about these two cases, and he discovers why when one moment he is in the Park and the next he is on an unfamiliar beach rescuing a woman from a creature straight out of a horror movie!

Stunned by the wild tale Marina tells him and the evidence surrounding them, Mike soon learns that everything she says is true—magic does exist—and he is no longer on Earth. Marina and Mike must work together to save the Isle of Magic and the rest of the kingdoms, but as the Sea Witch's evil spreads, they know they cannot stop her alone…

PROLOGUE

"I can't," the old man mumbled, shaking his head in distress. "My magic will not work against the Queen. We are bound. No, no… the Queen is too powerful."

"Oray," the queen called from the doorway of their private study.

The King of the Isle of Magic looked up from where he was sitting behind the beautifully carved wood desk. His eyes were glazed with an ink-black film.

With a frown, the Queen stepped into the darkened room. She waved her hand and the blinds slid back. Oray rose from his seat with an animalistic snarl. The Queen's hand froze in midair at the uncharacteristic sound.

"Isha," the Queen quietly called, never taking her eyes off of her husband. She saw only a reflection of herself in his black eyes, not the warm, loving, and compassionate man who had once inhabited his body.

"I see it, Your Majesty," Isha quietly responded.

Oray reached down and picked up the black box he had been talking to. Clutching the small, rectangular case between his gnarled hands, he pushed the chair back, and stepped into the shadows. His hands shook as the power inside the container began to surge, hungry for Magika and Isha's magic. He knew what they were looking at—the box, his box. They wanted to take it from him and destroy it.

He would have given them the box if he could—but the dark magic that was wrapped around him made it impossible to surrender the small container. Instead, he protectively cradled it against his body.

"I command you to leave," Oray ordered in a trembling voice.

"Oray, you are ill. Give me the box, and I will take you back to our living quarters to rest," Magika requested in a gentle tone, stepping further into the room.

"This is not for you. It is my gift. No one else can have it," Oray replied.

"When did she return it to you, Oray? The Sea Witch is banned from the Isle of Magic. You know that. You promised you would tell me if she returned. Please, husband, give the container to me. I miss who you were. Whatever unnatural magic is in the box, it is killing you," Magika said, continuing to walk toward him.

Oray trembled. He wanted to give in to his wife's request. He missed her soft touch, the laughter in her voice, the love they felt for each other. She completed him….

No, she is trying to trick you, a voice hissed in his head.

Our love…, Oray started to argue before wincing at the intense pain that shot through his body.

… is an illusion. They are trying to destroy you. It is time. Call the Sea Witch, the voice commanded. *We will stop the deceit of the Queen and her followers.*

"Please, Oray," Magika pleaded, stopping less than a foot from him.

Oray blinked at his wife, bringing her face into focus as he automatically reached out to her when she extended her hand toward him. His lips parted on a hiss, and he stumbled back several steps. Oray stopped when he hit the bookshelf behind him.

"Sea Witch… It has… commanded me to call you," Oray said with a shudder. He bowed his head, struggling to hold onto the last of his sanity. "Magika… You must escape. It is too late. I cannot fight it any longer."

Magika stepped back in shock when the small box in his hands began to dissolve into a dark mist that swirled around him. Oray lifted his head to gaze at his wife in agony. His fight to keep the creature from attaching itself to his magic was draining him. His gaze moved to the young warrior who came up behind Magika.

"It is too late. I can only hope to contain him long enough for you to get our Queen to safety," Oray forced out past the blackness wrapped around his throat.

"NO!" Magika cried, reaching out again for her husband.

"You must escape, Your Majesty," Isha ordered, pulling her behind him. "By the magic of my sword, you will release the King."

Isha swung his glowing sword at the black mist, but Oray knew it was already too late. The box in his hand had changed and was reforming into a ghostly creature determined to enslave him. Tentacles of black clashed with Isha's sword. Golden sparks glowed before the magic contained in Isha's sword sizzled and hissed. The black essence greedily absorbed the additional magic.

Oray could feel the Sea Witch's connection with the alien life form. Deep down, he was amazed that the young girl, who he had known since she was born, had been able to fight against the evil force contained within the black essence. The link he had with it allowed him to see what had happened to Magna. The parallels to his own situation were terrifying.

She had been overpowered, the same as he had been, and she was still there, trapped within it. Yet, he could still feel the essence of the young girl hidden beneath the layers—hiding, seeking her freedom. As hard as he had fought to understand, to resist, and to contain the malevolent life form, it had still sucked him into its suffocating grasp.

"Heart as cold as ice, keep my soul safe behind its frozen wall. I command you to seal me now," Oray whispered the spell in a tortured voice.

"Oray, NO!" Magika cried, struggling to get to her husband.

Magika's grief-stricken cry pierced him for a moment before the spell took effect. Oray knew the only way to protect his kingdom—and what was left of him—was to cast a spell that only his Queen or the death of the entity could one day free him from. A dusting of ice formed over his skin, turning it a light blue color. He exhaled small puffs of warm breath before white crystals formed. Inside, the blood in his veins slowed until even it no longer flowed.

He was alive, yet not. His body was stiff, moving like a puppet on a string handled by an inexperienced puppeteer when pushed by the evil mass flowing around him. The emotions from his last second of awareness were frozen on his face. The last thing he would remember would be Magika's distraught face.

Oray was unaware of what happened next. In his frozen world, he was of no use to the creature. Nothing could touch him or control him now—not even the anguished cries of his beloved could penetrate the ice protecting his soul.

"Your Majesty, escape!" Isha shouted as he swung his spelled sword at the swirling bands.

He was forced to retreat when the black mass solidified and formed into a half dozen deadly sharp points. He sliced through three of them. His blade sparked as it passed through the mass that dissolved and reformed. He clenched the sword's hilt with both hands, trying different spells and striking again and again in an effort to find out what would temporarily stop the beast.

Behind him, he heard the Queen utter a powerful spell. Veins made of diamonds rose from the floor. The long tubular coils twisted and turned, creating a cage around the creature. Isha turned when he saw, out of the corner of his eye, a movement near the window. From the shadows, Magna appeared. Dressed in a gown of blood-red with her black hair flowing around her as if caught in gale force winds, she stepped out of a swirling dark mist.

Isha continued his retreat. Behind him, he could hear the Queen's footsteps as she fled to warn the other guards. He could already see thin cracks appearing in the diamond prison the Queen had formed around the creature. Reaching out, he gripped the handle of the door with one hand and held his sword pointed toward Magna with his other.

His gaze swept over the Sea Witch's face. Her skin was pale as moonlight, and her dark eyes held a haunted expression that looked too large for her gaunt face. Her lips were the color of a moonless night and slightly parted. She stared at him with unblinking eyes the color of ink.

"The time has come for the magic held within the Isle to belong to us," she said in a voice that echoed strangely in the room.

Isha's hand tightened on the sword. "I will see you buried in the darkest regions of the ocean before the Isle of Magic will ever belong to you, Sea Witch," Isha snarled in an icy tone.

Closing the door and locking it with a strong spell, he wrapped both hands around his sword. With a shout, he poured every ounce of his magic into the sword. Lifting it, he charged Magna.

She stood still, as if waiting for his blade to pierce her. The diamond walls exploded, creating a deafening noise. Isha felt the pain from the diamond shards as they struck him but ignored it. Slicing his sword through the air, he caught his breath when the end of the sharp blade was stopped by a thick, black tentacle less than an inch from Magna's delicate neck.

Isha cried in pain when another deadly band wrapped around his waist. The band lifted him off his feet while other bands encircled his arms and legs. His sword, still glowing with his magic, fell from his numb fingers. He struggled, but the bands gripping him felt like a giant's fist squeezing his body until he was sure his bones would snap.

Gasping for air, he watched Magna step forward and bend to pick up his sword. Isha tried to withdraw his magic from it, but the blackness was draining him. He slowly curled the fingers of his right hand in frustration.

"Mag…na," he gasped.

"You have no idea of the power we are dealing with, Isha," Magna informed him.

Isha blinked when Magna lifted his sword. He opened his fingers to prepare for her strike, but he was instead shocked when she placed the sword in his hand. Darkness blurred the edge of his vision as a serene smile appeared on her face.

"Sleep warrior," Magna murmured.

Isha's lips parted on a gasp. He could feel the spell burning through his body like a flash fire. His features hardened until he was no longer a living, breathing entity but a stone statue in the image of the great warrior that he once was.

~

Marina Fae kicked at a pebble along her path and watched it bounce until it rolled to a stop against the vine covered walls of the palace. Shouldering her bow, a mischievous grin lit her face. She glanced around before lifting her arms up and wiggling her fingers. The vines hanging down from the tree on the other side of the wall spiraled down and wrapped around her wrists. A moment later, she was lowered to the ground on the other side of the wall.

Turning to face the tree, she did a brief curtsy. "Thank you, Mr. Tree," she laughed.

She turned and started cutting through the large garden surrounding the palace. Technically, she should have gone through the front gates, but she never did. One advantage of being the younger sister of the Captain of the Guard: everyone knew who she was.

Humming under her breath, she gripped her bow and took off at a slight jog along the winding path that cut through the huge garden maze. She was excited. Isha was supposed to return to their village today. She would surprise him at the palace—and just make sure he hadn't forgotten that he said he'd be home.

The annual Festival of Lights this weekend was a very special time in their village. Because the village was farther inland than the palace, which was closer to the sea, the mountains came alive once a year with the blooming of the Nightstar flowers. The blossoms would open, and the glowing seeds within would float up into the trees, lighting the forest with color. The villagers' voices would rise in song and spread their magic on the breeze to mix with the floating seeds. It truly was a magical night and one that she loved to witness.

Marina's steps slowed when she heard the sound of shouting and a scream that was cut short. She stumbled when the ground shook under her feet from a loud explosion that ripped through the air. To steady herself, she reached out and wrapped her left hand around the thick branch of one of the tall bushes that hedged the maze. She was almost to the exit near the main gardens to the right of the palace's front entrance.

Releasing the branch, she whispered to her bow. She could feel the string grow taut as she woke the magic within the bow. She moved forward in concern when she heard the Queen's voice rise above the shouts, cries, and screams.

A feeling of concern flooded Marina. She couldn't help thinking in an oddly disconnected way that she had never heard the Queen's voice raised in anger before. She had only taken a few steps forward when she caught her breath in surprise. Thick bands of magic swirled around her like a turbulent river, rushing toward the area where she had heard the Queen's voice. The pure beauty and power of the flowing colors took Marina's breath away.

Spying the exit from the maze, Marina put on a burst of speed. She slid to a stop when she cleared the last hedge. Her lips parted in horrified awe. On the front steps of the palace stood a slender woman. All around her, a dark mist twisted and churned. The woman looked as if she was made of the black essence.

"Sea Witch!" Marina whispered, her gaze glued to Magna.

"I command you to stop, Magna! As Queen of the Isle of Magic, I sentence you to death for your deceit and traitorous acts," Magika declared, lifting her hands.

"You cannot stop me. I now control the Isle of Magic and all the powers of this kingdom," Magna replied, her voice strangely flat.

"You are wrong, Magna. Whatever evil magic you have summoned, it is not from this world. Think of the damage you are doing," Magika responded in a cold voice.

"Magna!"

Marina turned to see Kell and Seline, Magna's parents, appear—the Queen must have summoned them. Hope rushed through Marina. Surely the pleas of the Sea Witch's parents would be able to touch their daughter.

"Think of your family, Magna," the Queen said.

Marina's gaze anxiously turned back to the Queen. A soft hiss slipped from her lips when she realized what the Queen was doing. Queen Magika was weaving a spell in her words and using Magna's parents to distract the Sea Witch.

Marina had never seen such pure and beautiful magic woven so tightly —so precisely. The ability to see magic was one of her talents. She had inherited her gift from her grandmother who had cautioned her to keep the ability to herself.

'No one else has the gift like you and I, Marina,' her grandmother told her when she was barely ten years old. *'Except perhaps the Queen and King. There isn't much use for the ability to see magic—except when you need to. Keep this little secret. You never know when it might come in handy,'* her grandmother had added with a wink.

Now, she watched the threads reaching out toward Magna. The magic was subtle, woven in the words the Queen spoke. Marina turned to focus her attention on Magna again. Was Magna able to see the magic? How would she react toward her parents?

Marina's mouth dropped open when the black essence surrounding Magna reached greedily for the hidden strands of magic. The Queen cried out in pain as the bands devoured the magical threads. Marina could see the malevolent mist greedily absorbing the Queen's magic—and growing stronger!

"Magna, no!" Kell shouted, stepping forward and placing himself between the Queen and his daughter. "Let us help you. Please, I beg of you. Give yourself up, and we will help you."

The expression on Magna's face softened, her lips parted, and for a moment Marina thought the Sea Witch would give in. Even from several yards away, Marina could see the conflict on the other woman's face. The indecision lasted no more than a second before her expression hardened.

"Watch out!" Marina cried, lifting her hand in warning.

She saw the change in the mist. In horror, she helplessly watched as two long tentacles shot out. The bands wrapped around Kell. Magna's mother, Seline, lifted her glowing hands while her lips moved, weaving a deadly spell to stop her daughter's attack. A wave of mist swept over Seline, hardening her features to stone and freezing the incomplete spell on her lips.

Magic unlike anything Marina had ever seen before rose up around those standing in the courtyard. All around her, the features of the Queen's guards and the few servants who had fled outside began to freeze and harden. Even Queen Magika was not immune to the horrifying mist turning her people to stone.

Marina frantically swept her gaze across the sea of faces, searching for her brother. She needed to find him. Surely Isha could feel the danger to the Queen and would come to her assistance—unless, she thought with a growing panic, he was protecting the King.

"Mr. Bow, I need arrows," Marina ordered, lifting the bow in her hand and drawing the bowstring.

"Isha!" the Queen cried, fighting to keep the black mist from enveloping her.

"He is lost to you, my Queen, just as everyone who resists me will be," the Sea Witch informed her, slowly descending the steps.

"What magic is this?" Magika demanded, her voice shaken as the circle around her grew smaller and smaller.

"It isn't magic. It is something far more powerful, more deadly, more horrifying than anything magic could create," Magna replied in a voice that barely carried on the wind.

Marina's fingers trembled and she lowered the bow in her hand. Her eyes widened as pain and grief swept through her. Behind Magna, Marina saw a man appear. He walked with stiff, jerky movements. His face, shimmering with a film of ice in the light, was devoid of all emotion, as if his body was there but that was all. Behind the King, the perfectly carved stone statue of her brother Isha, his magical sword still firmly held in his hand, floated past the King on a wave of the black mist. Marina released a broken cry of denial.

The Queen's anguished cry mixed with Marina's. Rage pierced the bubble of horror that surrounded her and her jaw tightened in determination. Lifting her bow, she didn't hesitate this time. She released the magical arrow. The fire burning through her veins increased when she saw the black bands swirling around Magna rise up to devour her arrow.

Marina's eyes narrowed, and she hissed out in fury. Reaching over her shoulder, she pulled an arrow from her quiver. If the creature fed on magic, she would see how it liked non-magical elements. Nocking the arrow, she pulled the bowstring back and whispered to her bow.

"Let my aim be true, Mr. Bow," she murmured.

Her fingers parted, releasing the string. The arrow flew through the air. The black bands reached greedily for the wooden shaft, but the arrow curved, dodging the tentacles that were trying to stop it. Magna turned at the last second, the tip of the arrow cutting a thin, deep cut along the bicep of her left arm.

Queen Magika turned and saw her. "Marina, you have to warn the kingdom...," Magika cried out seconds before the dark mist covered her and her body grew stiff.

"Stop her!" Magna snarled, grasping her injured arm with her other hand.

Marina lurched back several steps when the dark mass began to take shape. Massive creatures grew and solidified out of the bands. Their eyes glowed an eerie red while long, shiny, black fangs lengthened from their upper jaws. The black beasts had long snouts with a series of ridges that stopped between their eyes. Stiff spines rose from the top of their skulls and ran the length of their back down to their long, whip-like tails. Their four legs, each with massive paws and sharp claws dug into the soft grassy areas of the garden, which was littered with the petrified bodies of the palace's soldiers, servants, and the Queen.

Marina stumbled back toward the entrance to the maze, drawing another arrow from her quiver. Her hands remained steady, even as she drew in an uneven breath. These were not creatures of any magic she had ever seen before. Her mind flashed back to what the Queen had said to Magna. *'...it is not from this world. Think of the damage...'*

Lifting her chin, she pulled the bowstring back and breathed deeply when the beast closest to her snarled and took a step forward.

"Let's see if you are real," she said.

She whispered a spell. A dark blue film coated the tip of her arrow. Opening her fingers, she released the string as the beast leaped forward. Marina didn't wait to see if the arrow did its work or not. She turned and fled back into the maze.

CHAPTER ONE

Yachats, Oregon

"Mike! You have company," Patty called from the reception area.

Mike grimaced and wiped at the damp stain on his shirt where he'd spilled his coffee. It was going to be one of those days; he could feel it. It started out with his sister, Ruth, calling at an ungodly hour to inform him that she would be coming by for a visit. He could thank his birthday for that wonderful occasion.

"Just a minute," Mike answered, dropping the file folder on his desk.

He placed the cup of coffee he had picked up at the café down the street on a folded paper towel that showed the evidence of his spillage from the days before. Hell, who was he kidding, the whole week had been one mishap after another. With a shake of his head, he grabbed a crumpled napkin from the bag of bagels he had added to his order at the last minute.

"I got you an Everything bagel," Mike grunted, not looking up when he heard the footsteps stop outside the door.

"Thank you, but I've already eaten," an unfamiliar voice replied.

"Oh, hey Mike, did you remember the cream cheese this time?" Patty asked, peering around the slender Asian man watching him with a slightly amused expression.

"Yeah, I got extra," Mike replied, absently wiping at the wet spot on his dark blue dress shirt. "Can I help you?"

Mike ran his gaze over the man, quickly picking out and storing details: early 30s, approximately five feet ten inches, brown eyes, thin scar near his left eye. The creases pressed into his dress slacks, the polished black shoes, and the precision cut of his hair indicated he was military or former military. The man's gaze was taking in everything about Mike and his office, and Mike figured that made him Military Intelligence.

"Yes," came the short reply.

"I forgot your cappuccino, Patty. Why don't you go get it? I'll cover the phones," Mike suggested, holding out the bag with the bagels in it.

"Are you sure?" Patty asked, briefly glancing at the man who had stepped aside to allow her to enter.

Mike's lips twitched when Patty jerked her eyes as if trying to convey a secret message to him. "I'm sure," he replied in a dry tone.

"Oh, okay. Well, I won't be but a few minutes. If you need me, just call," Patty said, clutching the bag to her chest and turning to look up at their guest. "The café is like, right next door. The walls are thin—really thin, as in tissue paper thin if you know what I mean."

"Patty, go," Mike ordered in exasperation.

"Geez, I'm going," Patty muttered.

Mike remained standing until he heard the bell on the front door chime before he waved a hand to the seat across from him. He waited for the man to sit down before he took his seat. Gathering up the photographs that had spilled out of the file folder he dropped earlier, he tucked them back in and set it aside before sitting back in his chair.

"Now, what can I do for you Mr...," Mike began.

"Tanaka—Agent Asahi Tanaka, CIA," Asahi replied, reaching into the inside pocket of his jacket and pulling out his identification.

Mike leaned forward and took the slim leather wallet. Opening it, he scanned the credentials inside before closing the wallet and handing it back. Asahi returned the wallet to his pocket.

"So, what brings the CIA to Yachats, Oregon?" Mike asked.

"The file you have on your desk, Detective Hallbrook," Asahi replied.

Mike's gaze immediately went to the creased, coffee-stained folder. He needed to replace it. He'd been carrying this one around so much that it was almost worn out. He pressed his lips together and looked up at the man sitting across from him.

"What does the disappearance of two women have to do with the CIA?" Mike asked, clasping his hands together and forming a steeple with his two index fingers. "I could understand the FBI, but the CIA? That is pushing it, unless you think that Carly Tate and Jenny Ackerly were spies working for a foreign government."

Asahi's gaze moved from Mike to the file and back again. His lips pursed together for a moment before he relaxed, and his expression became unreadable. Mike had no doubt that this man spent more time out in the field than pushing papers.

"I'm not at liberty to explain, but yes, there is an interest in their disappearance," Asahi said with a slight bow of his head.

Mike leaned forward, resting his arms on his desk. A frown creased his brow as he thought about what the two women could have done to bring them to the attention of the CIA. Everything and everyone he talked to made him think that Carly and Jenny were just two ordinary

U.S. citizens who happened to know each other and be in the same place when they disappeared.

"If you aren't at liberty to tell me, then why are you here?" Mike sarcastically asked.

"You've been studying this case for a while," Asahi said.

"Since I took over here," Mike replied with a nod.

"Have you discovered anything... unusual about their disappearance?" Asahi inquired.

Mike didn't miss the way Asahi's eyes flickered to the file and back again. The man wanted to look at it. Mike could feel it in his bones. Curious, he placed his left hand on the file and pushed it toward the agent.

"Why don't you tell me?" Mike suggested.

They locked gazes for a brief moment before Asahi reached out to the take the file. Mike held the file long enough for Asahi to know that the information wouldn't come without a price. There was a brief flash of annoyance in Asahi's eyes.

"The information is need-to-know only," Asahi explained in a quiet voice.

Mike raised an eyebrow. "I need to know," he responded with a wry smile.

"How long have you lived in Yachats, Detective Hallbrook?" Asahi asked, pulling the folder toward him and opening it when Mike released it and sat back in his chair again.

"A couple of years," Mike replied. "Why?"

"Have you noticed anything unusual during the time you've lived here?" Asahi asked, slowly thumbing the notes and documents that Mike had collected.

"Define strange," Mike said dryly. "We have our share of unusual individuals who live in the area, but no one I would classify as dangerous."

"Dangerous is not necessarily what I am searching for," Asahi replied, pausing on a handwritten document comparing Carly and Jenny's disappearance. "May I have a copy of this file?"

"What in the hell is going on, Agent Tanaka?" Mike demanded.

Asahi looked up at Mike. His gaze was deadly serious. Mike's stomach clenched when the man hesitated and closed the file.

"Aliens," Asahi said at the same time as the front door chimed.

"Mike, I'm back! Did we get any phone calls? Is that weir… Oh, he's still here," Patty said, stopping in the doorway.

Mike rose at the same time as Asahi. They gazed at each other for a moment. Mike wondered if he'd heard the man correctly while Asahi waited for Mike's response to his request for copies.

"I was just leaving," Asahi stated, holding out the file.

"Patty can make you a copy of the files and send them to you," Mike said, lost in thought even as he reached for the file.

"Thank you. I will leave my information with her," Asahi replied, stepping around the chair

Mike looked down at the file in his hand. He could feel his head starting to shake in disbelief. He looked up as Asahi started to step through the door.

"Tanaka…," Mike called.

Asahi turned and looked back at Mike. He studied the other man's closed expression.

"Yes."

"Are you serious?" Mike asked.

"Completely. Have a good day, Detective Hallbrook. I'm sure we will meet again," Asahi said before turning and leaving.

Mike stood by his desk, his gaze blindly fixed on the empty doorway. It wasn't until he noticed Patty's return that he shook his head and sank down in his chair again. He looked up when she stopped in front of the desk.

"Are you shitting me? CIA? What the hell is going on?" Patty breathed.

Mike shook his head. "When you find out, let me know," he wryly retorted. "Can you...?"

"Yeah, he gave me his info," Patty said, anticipating what he was about to ask her to do. She picked up the file and shook her head in awe. "Who would have thought there would be so much excitement in this sleepy little town!"

Mike watched Patty turn and walk out the door. He knew that half the town would know about Agent Tanaka's visit by dinner. The rest would know by morning. Rising out of his seat, Mike grabbed his coffee and stepped around the desk. It was a good thing he hadn't removed his jacket this morning.

"Patty, I'm going out for a while," he yelled, heading for the back door of the police station.

Pushing the door open, he stepped outside. The thin layer of morning fog had settled into a dense curtain. A grim smile lifted the corner of his mouth. No fishing today; it looked like a good day to pay a visit to someone who had lived here all their life and knew both women.

Turning left, Mike decided it would be safer to walk than drive. It would also give him time to absorb what Tanaka had said. The guy asked if he had noticed anything unusual—besides the disappearance of the two women.

"Only some crazy CIA agent who thinks that aliens or monsters might actually exist," Mike muttered with a shake of his head.

Mike paused on the sidewalk outside of the bar that was popular with the locals. It was located at the entrance to one of the marinas favored by the fishermen in the area. Old trawlers lined the docks. They were a stark contrast to the newer, more expensive pleasure crafts located at the city's marina.

"Ross Galloway?" Mike asked an old man exiting the bar.

"Inside," the man said.

"Don't drive," Mike warned when he smelled the beer on the old man's breath.

"Can't, truck broke down," the man mumbled.

Mike started to groan. It wasn't even ten o'clock in the morning yet. The curse on his lips died when he saw an old woman in a red coat step around the corner. The old man perked up and wobbled towards her.

He listened as the woman lovingly chided the man before wrapping her arm around his waist. Mike watched as the two disappear into the fog. Drawing in a deep breath and releasing it, he returned his attention to his mission. He pulled the door open and stepped into the warm interior of the bar.

Even though it was early, the place had nearly a dozen people sitting around, shooting the breeze with each other, eating, or playing pool. The smell of bacon made his stomach growl, reminding him that he had grabbed his coffee, but Patty had commandeered the extra bagel he purchased earlier. Glancing around the dim interior, his gaze stopped on Ross Galloway sitting at a table near the back.

Mike strode through the room, nodding to those who called out a greeting. Ross looked up from where he was sitting and scowled when he saw Mike heading his way. Ignoring the frown, Mike pulled out the chair across from Ross and sat down.

"Hey, Mike. What'll you be having?" Dorothy asked from behind the bar.

"Two eggs over medium, bacon, hash browns, and whole wheat… and a coffee," Mike replied before turning his attention to Ross.

Ross picked up his fork and stabbed at the scrambled eggs on his plate. Ross was about the same age as Mike, with a stocky, muscular body and dark shaggy hair that was as wild as Ross's reputation. Mike sat back in his seat when Dorothy brought his coffee out.

"Thank you," Mike said with an appreciative smile.

"No problem. More coffee, Ross?" Dorothy asked.

Ross grunted and pushed his cup closer to the coffee pot that Dorothy was holding. He muttered a thanks under his breath. Mike sat forward when Dorothy walked off. He cradled his coffee cup between his hands, staring at the dark brown liquid.

"I told you, I didn't do anything," Ross finally said.

"I know," Mike replied.

Ross lifted his head and studied Mike's face for a moment before he resumed eating his breakfast. "So, why are you here then?" he asked in a blunt tone.

"I was hungry," Mike replied.

Ross shot him a look that told Mike he didn't believe him. Amusement swept through Mike when he thought of what Ross's expression would be like if he asked the man if he'd ever seen any aliens hanging around. As much as he wanted to dismiss Tanaka's visit as a ludicrous joke, he couldn't. The man had been far too serious.

"Here you go, hun. Do you need anything else?" Dorothy asked, placing Mike's food on the table in front of him.

"No, this is fine. Thanks, Dorothy," Mike replied.

"I'll bring more coffee in a few. You doing okay, Ross?" Dorothy asked.

"I'm good. Thanks, Dorothy," Ross said.

Mike waited for Dorothy to walk away before he started eating. The food was hot and the coffee strong. Mike didn't say anything at first. He often found that silence could do two things: give a man time to think or allow the other man time to stew. As the silence grew, Mike decided Ross was a thinker—which surprised him. He honestly thought the other man was more emotional and more likely to react than think.

Dorothy came by and refilled both of their cups, and both men finished eating before Mike spoke. Picking up his cup, he held it between his hands as he thought about how he should phrase his question. Each question he came up with sounded even more ridiculous than the one before.

"If you want to know something, just spit it out; that usually works," Ross suggested.

Mike looked up from his coffee to see Ross gazing at him with a wary expression. "Have you ever noticed anything strange around here?" he asked.

Ross raised one eyebrow and had an expression that asked Mike if he was shitting him. Mike grimaced. That wasn't what he'd planned to ask at all—or at least, not in those exact words.

"Well, let's see. Two women disappear, both talked to me, the cops keep sniffing around—no, nothing strange. Why do you ask?" Ross answered in a dry tone.

Mike set his coffee cup down on the table before running a hand over his face. He couldn't blame Ross for being slightly sarcastic. Hell, he would be too if he had been in Ross's position.

"You've lived here your whole life, right?" Mike countered, sitting forward and resting his elbows on the table.

"So," Ross replied.

Mike gritted his teeth in frustration. "So, have you ever noticed anything strange—weird—possibly extraterrestrial, even. Any unexplained anomalies, creatures, or things," he bit out.

Ross's expression changed from defiant to confused. "Anomalies—like Bigfoot or a mermaid?" he asked with an incredulous expression.

A scowl darkened Mike's face. "No, I'm not talking Bigfoot or mermaids—well, maybe. Have you seen anything that may not be normal?" he snapped in a low voice.

Ross nodded and glanced around him before leaning forward. Mike's fingers tightened on his coffee cup. He shot a quick look to make sure they couldn't be overheard before he leaned closer to Ross.

"I heard about this really strange detective who was asking dumbass questions about UFO's," Ross murmured.

Mike jolted back when Ross started laughing. The flash of anger turned into a chuckle of appreciation when Ross shot him a good-natured grin. Shaking his head, he lifted his coffee and finished it off.

"Do you guys need anything else?" Dorothy asked, coming up from behind Mike.

"Naw, tell Dennis the food was good as usual," Ross replied, pulling his wallet out of his pocket.

"You're just saying that so he doesn't kick your ass out of here," Dorothy teased, taking the twenty Ross was holding out.

"I'll take my bill as well, Dorothy," Mike said.

"Did you ever find out what happened to those two missing women? I have to tell you, it gives me the creeps thinking there might be a murderer on the loose around here," Dorothy commented.

"The cases are still open," Mike said, pulling out the money for his breakfast. "Keep the change."

"A customer after my own heart," Dorothy cheerfully replied with a quick grin at Ross.

Ross rose from his seat and shot a pained look at Mike. "Make the poor fisherman look bad," he said.

Dorothy shook her head. "I've seen your boat, Ross. I almost feel guilty taking your money—almost," she chuckled as she walked away.

"Yeah, tell me about it," Ross muttered. "Do you have anything else to ask me?"

"No—just… if you see or hear about anything unusual, please let me know," Mike said, rising out of his chair.

"If I see Bigfoot, I'll point you to him. If I see a mermaid, it might take me a while to report her if she's hot," Ross chuckled.

"I'll make a note of that," Mike dryly replied.

Mike followed Ross out of the pub. The morning fog had cleared, and he blinked as his eyes adjusted to the sudden brightness. He watched Ross turn and walk down to the docks.

Drawing in a deep breath, he shook his head. He automatically reached down when he felt his cell phone vibrate. Pulling it out of his back pocket, he released a groan at the message that flashed across the screen.

Happy birthday, baby brother. I'll be there around seven tonight. I'd love some of your homemade spaghetti, but since it's your birthday, I guess you'll have to settle for my famous peanut butter and jelly sandwiches.
Love ya, Ruth.

He quickly typed a reply. The immediate response of hearts and happy faces filled up the screen. He loved his sister, but she had to be the worst cook in the world. He never did have the heart to tell her that even her peanut butter and jelly sandwiches weren't all that great. It looked like he would be making a grocery store run on the way home this afternoon.

He was just about to shove his cell phone back into his pocket when it vibrated again. This time it was Patty. There was a reported break-in at one of the residences down by the cove. His plan to take a ride out to Yachats State Park today would have to wait another day. With a sigh, Mike started walking back along the sidewalk to the police station.

CHAPTER TWO

Later that night, Mike lifted the lid off the simmering pot of spaghetti sauce, picked up the spoon, and stirred. The pasta was finished, salads made, and garlic bread sliced. He glanced at the clock—six fifty-eight. Ruth should be here any minute.

Sure enough, the sound of a brisk knock on the door told him his big sister had arrived for the weekend. He placed the spoon on the counter next to the stove and turned off the burner. Pulling free the dish towel he had tucked into the waistband of his jeans, he placed it on the counter as well. A frown creased his brow when he heard Ruth knock again, this time louder than before.

"The door's unlocked," he called as he exited the kitchen and headed across the living room to the front door. He gripped the doorknob, twisted it, and pulled the door open. "Since when do you…."

"Happy Birthday, baby brother!" Ruth announced with a huge grin.

"What the fuck?!" Mike growled, raising his arms automatically when Ruth lifted the wiggling bundle in her arms.

"Happy Birthday!" Ruth grinned, pushing past him. "I have his bed and toys out in the back of my car. You can get them while I set the table. Oh, God! That smells so good. I'm starving."

"No, no, no, no, n...," Mike was saying before he ended up with a tongue in his mouth.

"Did you make....? Yes! Your homemade ranch dressing. I absolutely adore you!" Ruth said from the kitchen.

Mike stood there trying to glare at his sister. It was hard to do when he had to keep moving his head to avoid the tongue trying to find a way down his throat. Tucking the Golden Retriever puppy under his arm, he winced when it began chewing on his finger.

"Ruth!" Mike growled in frustration. "Please tell me you did not buy me a dog."

Ruth peeked around the corner. "No, I did not buy you a dog," she said with a sweet smile.

Her response stopped Mike in his tracks. He looked down at the golden body. A huge dark blue bow was attached to the puppy's collar with the words *Happy Birthday, baby brother* printed on it. The puppy looked up at him with eyes the color of melted chocolate, and he could feel its tail knocking against his side.

"Then explain this," he demanded, absently scratching the puppy's chin.

"I didn't buy him. He was given to me, and I am giving him to you," Ruth stated with a serene smile.

"Semantics. I'm not one of your legal documents, damn it! You know what I meant," Mike said, walking into the kitchen.

"Where are the napkins?" Ruth asked, opening cabinets and peering inside.

"Use paper towels, they work just as good," Mike replied in exasperation. "I don't want a dog."

Ruth paused and looked at him. Mike could feel his jaw clench and knew he was about to start grinding his teeth. She had that innocent look on her face—the one that meant she was settling in for the kill.

"He is my present to you," she said in a soft, calm voice.

"I know… but, it—he—is a dog! Worse, it—he—is a puppy! Do you know what puppies do?" he demanded.

"Yes, I know very well what puppies do. In fact, if I remember correctly, they do the same thing that rats do," Ruth replied.

Mike cringed. Yep, she was moving in for the kill. One mistake! He'd made one mistake fifteen years ago and now it was coming back to bite him in the ass.

"You were sixteen. I thought you would like them," Mike grumbled.

"You gave me rats for my sixteenth birthday," she reminded him. "Not one, but two—a girl and a boy. Be grateful you only got one puppy, baby brother. My friend had fourteen more."

"God, why do women have such long memories?" Mike groaned, turning and holding the puppy up to his face.

"You have to admit, puppies have better smelling breath," Ruth chuckled.

"He smells like cake," Mike retorted.

"Yes, well, there is a reason for that," Ruth laughed.

Mike glanced down at the puppy that was now trying to wiggle out of his arms. "At least she gave me a boy," he informed the puppy before bending over and placing him on the floor. "This means we are even, right?"

Ruth paused and looked over her shoulder. "Oh hell, no. Not by a long shot. You have about thirty-two more paybacks before I write off that nightmare," she responded.

"I think we should be even now," he argued, grabbing a bowl for the spaghetti sauce. "I was able to give twelve of the baby rats away to friends, and let another ten go free, and you gave me two fish for my fifteenth birthday after mom and dad gave us a list of non-acceptable pets. Also, you know that this puppy is going to chew on half of my new furniture, god knows how many pairs of shoes, and leave enough puddles and poop to fertilize half of Lincoln county. I won't even mention the hazards facing my living room carpet until I get him housebroken!"

"Carpet is bad for your allergies and you were planning on replacing it anyway. Oh, alright. I'll think about it," Ruth conceded with a dramatic sigh.

"I don't have any problems with allergies," Mike scowled before his expression changed. "I made the homemade ranch dressing and extra sauce for you to take home," he added with a sly smile.

Ruth bit her lip and contemplated his bribe for a moment. "Well, I guess that is worth a few rats. Okay, we're even," she grudgingly replied.

"Thank you for small miracles!" Mike muttered, turning to hand Ruth the bowl of sauce. "By the way, thanks for driving up for my birthday, sis."

"We promised we would be there for each other, no matter how far away we live," Ruth said, gazing up at him.

Mike nodded. They had promised after losing both of their parents that they wouldn't forget how important family was—especially since it was just the two of them now. Mike winced and looked down at the puppy attacking his sock-covered foot.

And if there are two things that his sister is very tenacious about, it is keeping promises and never forgetting anything, he thought.

"I'll get the pasta," he said in a gruff voice.

"And cheese," Ruth reminded him, turning toward the table. "By the way, the reason Charlie Brown here smells like cake is because he ate the one I bought you on the way up here."

Mike paused with his hand on the refrigerator door and looked at Ruth in dismay. He shot a glance at the puppy that was now attacking the straw on the broom leaning in the corner of the kitchen before looking back at Ruth.

"Please tell me you purchased a kennel for him," he said.

Ruth shook her head. "Of course not! You know how I feel about caging animals," she replied.

Great! Just great! he thought with a wince when the broom fell with a clatter and scared the puppy, which took off towards the living room.

Later that night, Mike lay in bed staring up at the ceiling, absently scratching Charlie behind his ear. The pup didn't whine when he placed him on the folded blanket on the floor next to his side of the bed. No, the damn thing had stared at him with huge, unblinking eyes and a soulful, lost look.

He had tried rolling over so his back was to the puppy, but he could feel the pup's eyes drilling a hole between his shoulder blades. Rolling over, he had finally given up and growled for the pup to join him. Of course, it took another ten minutes after that to make Charlie stop licking him and settle down.

Mike drew in a deep breath and released it. He was tired, but his mind was buzzing with everything that he and Ruth had talked about. Mostly, he thought about how the carefully laid plans for his life had changed.

It had been almost two years since he gave up his commission in the Air Force. He had planned to stay in and serve his twenty years before retiring to do some traveling. Somewhere in the mix he figured he'd get married if he met the right woman, but he was in no hurry.

With eight years of service, he was almost halfway to his goal. Everything changed the night he received Ruth's urgent phone call. Their dad, a career Air Force Colonel, had collapsed. Family needed family and when their dad was diagnosed with terminal brain cancer, he had returned home. What neither he nor Ruth expected was that they would be burying both their parents within two weeks of each other, their father from the cancer and their mother from a stroke, less than seven months after Mike had come home.

Mike knew Ruth felt guilty about his leaving the service. The thing was, no one knew exactly how long their dad would last, or that their mom would die so soon afterward. Ultimately, the decision had been his to make, and he realized afterward that it had been the right one. He had been trying to follow in their dad's footsteps, but in reality, he had grown tired of the confines of the military and was ready for a change.

The position at the Yachats Police Department was obtained through a friend at his mom's funeral. Two weeks later, he and Ruth had finished packing up all of their parents' belongings and placed the house in Sacramento, California on the market. Afterward, he had headed north. He'd considered Yachats as a place where he could stop and think, a layover for where he was going to go next. With the disappearance of Carly Tate and then Jenny Ackerly, he knew he wouldn't be going anywhere else—at least not until he found out what had happened to them. He never left anything undone, and he had promised Jenny he would bring Carly home. Now, he felt like he owed it to Jenny.

Rolling over, he wrapped his arm around the golden fur-ball that was now snoring. A chuckle escaped him. He would have preferred a different warm body in bed next to him on his birthday but, as a second choice, it was better than a cold pillow, he decided.

Scratching the pup's belly, he released a huge yawn and felt the last of the tension leave his body. "Goodnight, Charlie Brown," he whispered in the dark as his mind finally shut down enough for sleep to overtake him.

CHAPTER THREE

Four months later:

"Not now, Charlie," Mike muttered.

Taking the ball Charlie had dropped on the case documents he was reviewing, Mike tossed it across the living room. He ignored Charlie's happy bark and the sound of the dog's nails against his newly installed tile flooring. Leaning forward, he turned over the paper he had just re-read for the hundredth time and began reading the next page.

"Come on, talk to me. Where are you? What happened to you?" he said in frustration.

He turned another page. He knew it was stupid to talk to a couple of pictures, but he didn't care. It wasn't as if anyone could hear him except for Charlie. He leaned back on the couch and ran a tired hand through his hair. He'd been staring at the damn file for over two hours.

He wanted to blame it on Agent Tanaka's call late yesterday afternoon. He'd put the case file away for the last couple of months. Now, it was back out of the file drawer and nagging at him again. Tanaka said he was just checking in to see if Mike had discovered anything new.

"No, I have not discovered any evidence of aliens, mermaids, Bigfoot, or Santa Claus' summer residence," he had grunted into the phone.

Tanaka had not been amused. The sound of silence followed by a stiff thank you had pulled another groan from Mike. Yesterday had been a very trying day. Two teens had taken one of the yachts for a joy ride, there had been a fender-bender at the grocery store, and Charlie had watered Patty's fake fern tree in the front office again.

He'd spent almost an hour washing it off and hoped it would dry before Monday so that Patty wouldn't notice anything amiss with her prized, five-dollar yard sale decoration. Life was easier when Patty was in the office, at least she could help keep Charlie entertained and out of mischief for more than five minutes. Deciding he'd endured enough for the day, he had rounded up Charlie and headed home.

"Damn it, Charlie! I said…," Mike started to say before he snapped his mouth closed.

Charlie had trotted back over and dropped the purple squeaky ball on the papers scattered across the coffee table. The pup whined and placed his chin on Mike's knee. He chuckled at the pitiful look. Reaching over, he scratched Charlie behind the ear, earning a tail wag.

"I guess you are as tired of being cooped up as I am. How about we combine work and play, boy? We could go for a run and do a little field duty," Mike suggested.

Mike fell back against the back of the couch when Charlie enthusiastically agreed. Two large paws and a long tongue told Mike he'd better hurry if he was going to save the papers from being scattered across the living room floor after Charlie's hairy tail cleared off most of them on the first swipe.

Pushing Charlie off of his lap, Mike stood up and began collecting all the papers. He picked up one of the fallen pictures from under the coffee table. Standing straight, he studied the photograph. Carly Tate and Jenny Ackerly's smiling faces stared back at him. A strange sense of calm swept through him. It was almost as if the two women were telling him that everything would be alright.

He shook his head at the crazy thought that the women were trying to talk to him. He was losing his freaking mind. Gazing down at Charlie, Mike decided he needed some fresh air as much as the dog did! He bent over and stacked the rest of the papers and photos together and closed the file.

He looked at the calendar hanging on the wall. Today marked the one year anniversary of Jenny's disappearance. Shaking his head, he slid the file into a large envelope. He could always take it with him and go through it at the scene where both women's cars were found. Maybe some fresh air, a little exercise, and being on the scene would make something click. It wasn't as if he had anything more pressing to do. He had the entire weekend off.

Hell, if nothing else, he thought, watching Charlie hopping up and down off the couch in excitement, *I can try to wear Charlie out a little so I can get some work done.*

Grabbing his jacket and Charlie's leash off the coat rack near the front door, he pulled the door open. Charlie pushed by him, making short, happy growling sounds. Mike had to dodge the lethal tail before he could close and lock the door behind him.

"Let's go, boy," Mike said, grinning when Charlie jumped down the front steps and ran around the truck once before stopping at the driver's door.

Mike opened the door and waited for Charlie to scramble in before he slid in after the dog. Inserting the key into the ignition, he pressed the button to roll down the passenger window halfway. Charlie dropped his squeaky ball on the seat and stuck his head out the window.

"Watch the tail, boy," Mike grumbled, pushing on Charlie's hindquarters to make him sit. "That's much better."

Backing out of the driveway, Mike's switched his thoughts back to the information he had been reading over again before they left. He ran through what he knew about the two missing women again. They had been best friends since kindergarten and became roommates after graduating from high school. Carly worked at the local bank while Jenny was a teacher at the elementary school. The biggest coincidence between the two was when and where they disappeared, two years apart to the day.

Mike couldn't help but wonder if someone had been stalking the two women. He'd investigated to see if there were any drifters or residents who might have fit the pattern or appeared suspicious, but he'd come up with a blank. Hell, even Ross came up clean, which had surprised Mike.

Turning into the long entrance to Yachats State Park, Mike slowed down at the gate. He shifted the truck into park and pulled his wallet out of his front pocket.

"Hey, Mike. How are you doing today?" the ranger said after opening the window.

"Good, how about you, Marty?" Mike replied.

"Not bad, you here on personal or business?" Marty asked, looking at Mike's Annual State Park Pass.

"Both," Mike replied, taking his card back when Marty held it out to him.

"If you need anything, just call," Marty said.

Mike nodded, then paused. "You've been here a while haven't you, Marty?" he asked, gazing back at the other man.

"About six or seven years now," Marty replied, leaning on the windowsill.

"Have you ever seen or heard anything unusual?" Mike asked.

Marty shrugged. "There's always something unusual when you're in the woods. Can you be more specific?" he asked with a confused frown.

"I don't know, strange, unexplainable," Mike said.

"Like Bigfoot strange?" Marty asked.

Mike shook his head. "What is it with people and Bigfoot?" he scoffed with a deep sigh. "Okay, yes, like Bigfoot."

Marty looked thoughtful for a moment before he shook his head. "Naw. I've seen strange dancing lights. I figured it might be some type of methane gas balls. I've seen those before, down in the swamps, when I worked at the State Park in Louisiana. I've heard some strange noises, felt a minor quake or two, and the lights, but nothing like Bigfoot. I'd love to get a picture of him…."

Mike realized that this conversation was going south along with the floating gas balls when Marty started relating all the weird stuff he'd seen. Fortunately, Charlie decided they had stopped long enough and began to whine. Mike ran his hand down the dog's head when Charlie turned and gave him a lick.

"Thanks, Marty. I'll see you later," Mike said, cutting the other man off.

"See you, Mike. Bye Charlie," Marty said with a wave.

Charlie barked in Mike's ear. Mike shifted the truck into gear and eased off the brake. Pulling forward, he accelerated once they had cleared the speed bump. Charlie, happy that they were moving again, resumed his position as co-pilot. Mike chuckled at the pure enjoyment Charlie was getting from hanging his head out the window, his ears flapping in the breeze, and his nose going a million miles an hour.

"Let me know if you smell Bigfoot, okay, boy?" Mike instructed.

Ten minutes later, Mike was parked in the parking lot where Carly and Jenny's cars had been recovered. Through the windshield of his truck, he gazed at the forest ahead of him. The clouds were rolling in from the ocean, making it another dreary, overcast day, which was typical of the weather for the area. The parking lot was empty, leaving Mike to summarize that other would-be visitors had looked at the weather forecast before deciding to venture out. Turning off the engine, he sat in his car for several minutes looking out at the thick line of trees in front of him.

"Sometimes I think I need my head examined," he muttered under his breath, even as he reached for the dark brown jacket lying underneath Charlie on the seat next to him. Mike grinned when a cold nose pushed against his hand. "I know, I know. Nature calls and there are only a million trees to mark," he said, lifting his hand to scratch Charlie, who decided to lay down at the same time he tried to pick up his jacket. "I promised you a run today, no matter what, so no pooping out on me now that we are here. Let's go."

Mike pushed open the door and slid out of the truck. Charlie immediately stood up, his dark golden body quivering with excitement. Mike stood in front of the door, blocking the opening while he pulled on his jacket. Reaching between Charlie and the back of the seat, Mike grabbed the retractable leash. He grimaced when Charlie ran his tongue over his cheek.

"Thanks, dude," Mike muttered as he clipped the leash to Charlie's collar. He rubbed his cheek against the soft fabric lining the collar of his jacket. "Let's go, boy. I'll let you off once we get to the beach."

He stepped back so that Charlie could jump down and then closed the door. Pressing the lock, he turned and headed down the trail with Charlie trotting enthusiastically by his side. He used his free hand to pull up the collar of his jacket when it began to heavily mist and a gust of wind sent a trickle of cold water down his neck. Mike shook his head when Charlie just looked up with his tongue hanging out and wagged his tail.

"Don't look at me," Mike softly chuckled. "You can thank Mother Nature. She must know how much you love the water."

Mike tucked his left hand into the pocket of his leather jacket and focused on the path in front of him. Walking along the trail, his mind wandered as they stopped by every other tree so Charlie could sniff or leave his mark. After the fifth tree, Mike decided they'd never make it to the beach at the rate they were going.

Mike sighed as they navigated the uneven trail. His thoughts flashed back to his conversation with Ruth a few months before. He had encouraged Ruth to never give up on finding someone. He knew his sister was gun-shy after her marriage ended. Mike hadn't known much about Howard but, from the little he did know, he had to admit he was surprised that Ruth had seen anything in the guy. Ruth had a powerful personality. She was blunt like their dad and opinionated like their mother. When you put both of those traits together and mixed in a high IQ and a smart-ass sense of humor, it made it difficult to find someone who could keep up with her without feeling intimidated.

Of course, she had pointed out that at least she did try to find someone. That had shut him up. Now, it was just Ruth and him… and Charlie. His gaze flickered to the dog. Charlie had stopped to smell the base of yet another huge Douglas Fir that grew along the path.

"Okay, six times. That's the limit," Mike told the pup with a shake of his head. "Where in the hell you store that much pee is beyond me." Charlie looked up at him with a happy grin after making sure the tree was properly watered. "I don't know why I thought I could discover anything with you along except maybe how many gallons of pee a dog can hold in his bladder."

"Woof," Charlie responded before pulling on the leash.

"Okay, okay," Mike chuckled. "We'll head down to the beach. Maybe chasing a few sticks will make you feel better. I swear it's official—I've gone nuts. Now I'm talking to the dog, and he answers me. What's next, a woodland witch or a mermaid to tempt my heart?"

A shiver ran down his spine when Charlie whined. Shrugging his shoulders, Mike pushed his unease away as a sudden burst of energy flooded his body. A grin curved his lips as he reached down and unhooked the leash.

"I'll race you," he said, pocketing the leash and taking off down the crooked, uneven trail at an easy run. "First one on the beach has to clean the dishes tonight."

A husky laugh escaped him when Charlie darted ahead of him. Inhaling deeply, Mike breathed in the cold, damp air. It filled his lungs, energizing him. For the first time in over a year, he felt like his life was beginning to make sense again.

I just hope it is more than cleaning the dishes after Charlie licks them, he thought as they broke through the opening in the trees and onto the rocky shore.

Ten minutes and half-a-mile later, Mike slowed to a walk. Charlie ran circles around him, a large piece of driftwood in his mouth. Mike chuckled at the dog's antics. It felt good to be out and to run, even if it was only a short distance.

Breathing deeply, Mike enjoyed the mixture of cold air and salt. Typical of the weather along the coast, the sun was now shining. The saying *just wait five minutes and the weather will change* was never more true than along the coast of the Pacific Northwest.

Mike bent over and grabbed the stick from Charlie's jaws. The pup immediately let it go and danced back several steps in anticipation. Pulling his arm back, he threw the piece of wood. Charlie took off after it like a bullet. A second later, the laugh on Mike's lips turned to a muttered oath. Charlie's startled yelp and quick retreat to cower behind Mike proved to him that he wasn't hallucinating.

"What the hell?" Mike said under his breath.

In front of him, where the beach used to be had changed to a swirling whirlpool of color. Shock changed to a frown of concentration when the center of the whirlpool began to turn clear. Charlie's deep growl of warning came less than a second after the hair on the back of Mike's neck literally stood up from the electrical charge in the air.

Mike's internal warning bells started clamoring, and he couldn't help but briefly acknowledge that Tanaka's alien theory might have some merit to it after all! At the thought, he instinctively reached for the pistol in his hip holster. He flicked the snap open and quickly drew the pistol, holding it steady in both hands as he took a step closer to the anomaly. His eyes widened when he saw a woman twisting and falling to the ground. Her arm rose in a defensive move. It took less than a second to understand why when a massive black creature with three legs leaped to attack her.

The familiar recoil of his gun firing reverberated through him. He'd aimed for the center of the creature's forehead before lowering the gun to aim at its broad chest. With each shot, he took a determined step closer in an effort to reach the woman and get her to safety.

The black body crashed to the rock and sand strewn beach with enough force that Mike could feel the ground shake from the impact. The body skidded several feet before it came to a halt near the woman. The woman's head lifted, and she stared in shock at the dead creature.

Mike released a smothered curse when Charlie darted past him toward the woman. "Charlie, heel! Damn it, dog. Will you come here?" he ordered in a sharp voice.

He stepped closer and briefly looked down at the woman before his gaze moved to scan the area in case there were any more of the things waiting to attack. Once he was fairly confident there were no more, he turned his gaze back to the thing he'd just shot. Hell, it didn't even look like it was from Earth!

Shaken, he looked at the mahogany-haired woman gazing up at him in shock. He didn't know much about wildlife, but one thing he did know—the thing he'd just killed looked like something out of a science fiction or horror movie.

And so did the woman, he thought.

CHAPTER FOUR

An hour earlier on the Isle of Magic:

Drawing in a deep breath, Marina watched as one of the Sea Witch's guards dismounted. He squatted down, touching the ground before he glanced up and snarled. His sharp teeth snapped together in a savage string of twisted words that were difficult to understand, but the message was clear. She and her brother and sister had been found.

Marina rose up and pulled back on the bowstring. An arrow, blazing with magical energy appeared. She released the arrow just as the ogre rose to his feet. The arrow pierced his chest, disappearing completely inside him. Not waiting for his body to fall, she released a second arrow toward the other guard and a third, fourth, and fifth one into the Hellhound standing next to the first guard.

The bodies glowed for a moment as the powerful magic embedded in the arrows discharged. The fiery burst of energy created cracks of jagged red lines along their skin before their bodies turned to ash. All evidence of their presence was gone as the late afternoon breeze caught the dissolving flakes and carried them away.

Marina held her ground as the remaining Hellhounds swiveled around, watching the floating ash. She released her arrows as quickly as she could pull back on the bowstring. Fear gripped her. It took another three arrows to kill the second Hellhound before she could turn her attention to the third one. By then, it had narrowed in on her position.

Adrenaline poured through her when she saw it leap up onto the rocks below her. She shot an arrow into the beast's right shoulder, then turned and quickly scrambled over the large boulders to lead it away from her brother and sister's hiding place.

Jumping down, Marina bent her knees as she landed on the uneven rock below her and quickly slid down, falling the last six feet to the ground. Her feet dug into the ground, and she fell forward into a roll before coming back up on her feet.

She glanced over her shoulder when she heard the Hellhound's vicious snarl, watching as it twisted around in an attempt to follow her. Its right front leg had dissolved below the shoulder where she had shot it. It rolled off the boulder, hitting the ground with a hard thump.

A renewed wave of adrenaline flooded her as she took off through the woods and down the path. The uneven ground divided, one section leading back to her village, the other to the turbulent seas that surrounded the Isle of Magic. Unwilling to endanger the villagers any more than she already had, Marina turned toward the darker path.

Her heart pounded as she jumped over a fallen log. She turned as she landed, stumbling backwards, and fired another enchanted arrow. The Hellhound swerved, crashing into a huge tree as it avoided the blazing shaft. Marina turned on her heel as it lost its balance again. Even with three legs, the beast could run faster than she could once they were on open ground. She must make it to the beach where she could get a clear shot. A low branch in front of her lifted just enough to keep her from crawling to get under it. The beast was mere seconds behind her.

She could heard the sound of wood splintering, and the tree's moan as the Hellhound snapped the branch as if it were a twig.

"Please, let my aim be true Mr. Bow," she whispered as she ran.

Shielding her face with her arm, she pushed through the last veil of tangled vines covering the entrance to the rocky beach. Running across the sand and rock, she made it almost twenty yards when the loose rocks under her feet shifted, throwing her off balance when she tried to look behind her.

A sharp cry escaped her when her ankle twisted on the loose rocks, and she fell hard. Her gaze flew to where her bow landed several feet from where she lay sprawled on the uneven ground. She pushed up onto her elbow, biting her lip when pain radiated from her ankle. The Hellhound's loud snarl as it burst through the opening onto the beach sent a shaft of fear through her, and she twisted until she was facing it.

She watched as it slowly scanned the beach and locked onto her location. Raising her hand, she whispered a spell, calling for her bow to come to her. Her eyes widened, and she flinched when the beast released a loud roar as it tensed for an attack. She frantically searched for her bow when she did not feel it in her hand.

Dread filled her when she realized the spell she had woven had opened a portal behind her. In her haste, she had uttered the wrong words. This mistake would be the death of her. She cried in denial when the beast leaped toward her. Falling backwards, she watched as if in slow motion as the Hellhound's body left the ground.

Turning her head away, she tensed in preparation for the impact. She didn't see the Hellhound as it jerked and tumbled to the side, but she heard several loud explosions fill the air. Slowly opening her eyes, she stared in shock at the dead creature.

Her breath hiccuped as she lay twisted to the side. Mere inches from where she lay, the Hellhound's blank eyes stared at her. She jerked and shrieked when a cold, moist thing pressed against the heated skin of her neck. Turning her head, she was rewarded with a warm tongue across her cheek.

"Charlie, heel!" a deep voice commanded from behind her. "Damn it, dog. Will you come here?"

Marina turned, her eyes wide with disbelief as the face of a strange man suddenly came into view. His hands were raised as he cautiously stepped toward her. At first, she thought he was staring at her, but she quickly realized his eyes were on the Hellhound lying next to her.

She squeaked when the golden-haired beast suddenly blocked her vision. It whined and laid down next to her, resting its head on her chest. "Oh! I… good... beast," she stammered when it raised its head and suddenly licked her chin.

Marina nervously turned her attention back to the man. He looked down at her before his eyes flickered to the Hellhound again. He turned in a slow circle, studying the long beach with a confused frown on his face. He was silent for several long seconds as if he were processing what just happened. Marina didn't care; his confusion gave her a chance to catch her breath and study the man who saved her life.

She ran her gaze over his rugged face. His eyes were a clear blue, just like the sky on a cloudless day, and were framed by black lashes. His face was lean and tanned. He was wearing a black sweater that covered the firm column of his throat. The dark-brown leather jacket was open in front, and his strong hands were wrapped around a dark metal weapon of some type. She swallowed as she moved her gaze down to his flat stomach and lean hips encased in dark-blue material.

"What in the hell was that thing?" he demanded before he frowned at the golden-haired beast licking her hand. "Charlie, get over here."

Marina's lips twitched in unexpected amusement when the creature named Charlie lifted his head and wagged his tail but didn't move from her side. Gingerly sitting up, Marina raised a hand to push back the strands of her dark mahogany hair. It had come loose from the braid during her run. She grimaced when a long, wet tongue brushed her chin, but she didn't push the beast away from her. Instead, her fingers instinctively threaded through the long hair.

"It is a Hellhound. One of the Sea Witch's creations," Marina responded, motioning toward the Hellhound.

"Listen, are you okay? I saw you fall, then that thing jumped and...," he asked in a deep voice, his gaze moving from her face to the Hellhound and back again.

"Yes. Thank you for saving my life," Marina replied, stroking the golden-haired beast. "Where did you come from, and what magic did you use to kill it? The other ones took three of my arrows with one of my most powerful spells to do such a task."

"I.... Arrows? Spells?" the man paused and shook his head in confusion. "Where in the hell am I?"

Marina tilted her head to the side as she gazed up at him with a sudden feeling of dread. Something told her that the spell she cast did more than open a portal, it allowed something or, in this case, someone through who did not belong in her world. She had never opened a portal before—in fact, the only people she knew who might be powerful enough to open one were the Queen and King.

She didn't understand how she could have opened a cross-dimensional portal. She quickly dismissed that idea. While there was no denying that a spell more powerful than any she had ever created before had occurred, it didn't mean that this man came from another world. He was probably from one of the other kingdoms.

Whatever was the cause, Marina was thankful for his help. There was no denying that he had saved her life. A brief thought flashed through her mind that perhaps this man was the one her mother told them about. Marina looked up at the man again and dismissed that idea as well. She could not see any magic surrounding him. Even the weapon in his hand did not show a magical aura.

Bowing her head, she focused on the pain in her ankle. Her right ankle throbbed. It wasn't broken, but it was definitely very badly sprained. She leaned forward, spreading her hands above her ankle. Softly uttering a simple spell, she felt warmth begin to spread through the damaged tissue. Her healing magic was not as strong as that of her mother and sister, but it would have to do if she wanted to return to where she had left her brother and sister before darkness fell.

She would have to be careful. Her ankle would still be weak and tender. She couldn't afford to twist it again or run into any more of Magna's guards. She sighed in relief as the pain began to fade.

"You are on the Isle of Magic," Marina stated, testing her ankle before she slowly pushed Charlie back so she could rise to her feet. "Which Isle are you from?"

Marina knew immediately from the blank expression on the man's face that something was very wrong. Her gaze ran over him once more before moving to the beast staring up at her with warm, brown eyes. The sense of uncertainty returned with a vengeance. She looked back at the man and bit her lip.

"You are not from any of the Isles, are you?" she asked in a soft, hesitant voice as she studied the mix of emotions running across his face.

The man shook his head in a slow, measured movement. He returned her intent stare before looking around at the beach. His eyes paused on the Hellhound. She saw him swallow and lower the weapon in his hands. He carefully slipped it back into a black holster at his waist before he snapped his fingers. Charlie immediately went to his side and whined. She felt his gaze run over her again and knew he hadn't missed a thing when he looked back into her dark purple eyes.

"I think you need to start talking—now," he stated in a hard voice. "I want to know where in the hell I am, who you are, and what the hell that thing is."

Marina sighed and glanced at the darkening sky. With a muttered curse, she knew she didn't have much time or much of a choice; he would have to go with her. Turning, she walked over to her bow and picked it up.

"I'm sorry, Marina," the bow said.

"It isn't your fault, Mr. Bow. I should have held on to you better," she replied. "Let's take care of the Hellhound while we still can."

Turning, she pulled back on the bowstring. The string glowed with her magic, and she shot three arrows into the dead creature. In silence, she watched as the Hellhound glowed before turning to ash. Only when she was satisfied there was no evidence of the creature or her presence did she turn back to the pale-faced man watching her.

"My name is Marina Fae," she said. "I am the daughter of Ariness and Cornelia from the Village of Raines. We need to leave. It will be dark soon, and we are not safe here."

She turned on her heel and started walking back toward the forest. She glanced over her shoulder and paused when she saw that the man was still standing in the same place. She gripped the bow in her left hand and impatiently pushed her hair back when a long strand blew across her face.

"What the fuck are you?" the man asked in a hoarse voice.

"I am a witch, of course," Marina replied with a raised eyebrow. "Haven't you ever met one before?"

CHAPTER FIVE

Mike stared at the woman in shock before he slowly shook his head. "No, not a real one anyway," he tersely replied.

She tilted her head and frowned at him. "What other kind of witch is there?" she asked.

"Marina, that's what you said your name is, right? Would you please tell me what in the hell is going on?" Mike demanded.

"I will, but not here," she replied, taking a step toward him. "It is dangerous to be out in the open like this. One of the Sea Witch's creatures might still be around." She looked up at the sky again before looking back at him. "It will also be dark soon. We need to find a safe place for the night before the sun sets."

"The sun sets? It was morning just a few minutes ago back… where I'm from," Mike replied, waving his hand behind him.

He looked back down the empty beach again. He was trying to ignore the fact that the ocean was now almost the same color as the woman's eyes. It should have been blue, green, or almost black but not purple. Whoever heard of a purple ocean?!

He swung his head back toward her when he felt the touch of her hand on his arm. Marina gazed up at him with an intense look. Her face was tight with determination.

"What is your name?" she asked.

"What? Oh, yeah, sorry. My name is Mike Hallbrook," Mike replied. "Are your eyes really that color?"

A startled chuckle escaped her. She blinked and nodded her head. Mike caught the amused smile on her lips before it faded. She stared up at him with wide, serious eyes.

"Mike Hallbrook, I promise to tell you everything I know once we are safe. Please, trust me for now," she said in a quiet voice.

Mike hesitated. He couldn't help but look back at the spot where that thing had been just minutes earlier. It had been unlike anything he'd ever seen before. He gave a brief nod.

"I'll follow you for now, but I expect you to explain everything the second we stop wherever you think is a safe place," he bit out.

"Agreed," she said.

Mike watched her walk away. His gaze ran over her slender, almost boyish figure. *Not boyish—waif-like,* he thought as he began to follow her across the rocky beach to the tree line.

"Traitor," Mike muttered under his breath when Charlie trotted ahead of him to walk beside the woman.

Mike glanced around, noting and storing details even as his mind replayed what happened. A quick look over his shoulder back the way they had come showed massive cliffs rising out of the water, almost twice the height of those back home. Their sheer size reminded him of the cliffs he had seen at Big Bend National Park along the Rio Grande in Texas. He paused at the entrance to the forest and stared up at the sky. The distinctive shape of two moons could be seen, one closer to the planet than the other, but definitely two moons.

"Mike, come. It will be dark in less than an hour," Marina called in a quiet voice.

"I'm coming," he said, turning back around and pushing the loose vines out of his way. "I don't know where I'm going, but I'm coming."

The scene from the beach earlier played like a broken record in Mike's head as he followed Marina and Charlie. Each step seemed to increase the number of questions he had and emphasize the strangeness of the situation.

He gritted his teeth in frustration. More than once, Marina stopped and held up her hand. He could tell she was listening to the sounds around them before she started forward again.

Farther down the trail, they came to a spot where a limb the size of his thigh lay twisted and broken. Marina ran her hand over the broken area. Mike knew his mouth had dropped open when the ravaged pieces twisted and formed a knot.

"What did you do?" he asked, curious.

Marina shrugged and continued moving down the path. "My strongest gift of magic is with the trees and plants. Mr. Tree helped slow down the Hellhound as best he could. In doing so, he was damaged. Such damage, if not taken care of, can open a tree to predators that feed on the open wounds. Most of the time, nature must take its course, and the tree will survive and heal. Damage done by Magna's evil will fester, and the trees will die unless they are healed. I do what I can to protect them," Marina stated. "There is a tree not far from here where we can find shelter for the night. Darkness comes quickly, and we must hurry."

Mike silently nodded in acknowledgment. Following her in silence, he couldn't help but notice that she moved with grace. He blinked several times wondering if his eyes were playing tricks on him because she stepped so lightly it almost looked as if she were floating above the ground.

Her hair was a dark mahogany while her eyes were a dark purple. Something told him both were natural, especially after her reaction earlier when he asked about her eyes.

She was dressed in a long black sweater that stopped mid-thigh. She wore black leggings and black boots that reached her knees. He swallowed and watched Charlie duck under a log. It was obvious the pup had taken a liking to the woman.

'Marina' he silently corrected himself. *Daughter of Ariness and Cornelia from the Village of Raines. Don't forget she's a witch, of course, dumbass!*

He was still trying to get it through his head that she had shot magic arrows into a creature straight out of a horror film. The arrows had glowed before disappearing inside the beast. Then the whole thing had turned to ash. He wasn't even going to think about the fact that the bow could talk or the way she made the tree do that weird knot thing.

Hell, I'm still trying to wrap my head around that nightmare on the beach, he thought in exasperation.

Marina paused on the trail. He could see her indecision. Charlie whined and nudged her hand.

"What is it?" Mike asked.

She bit her lip. She gazed farther down the trail before turning to look at him. The flicker of uncertainty told him that there was something else going on.

"I left my brother and sister in the rocks not far from here. I told Geoff I would be back once I drew the Hellhounds away," she admitted.

"So, what is the problem? We go get them and get to this safe spot before dark," he replied.

She smiled and an expression of relief flickered through her unusual eyes. She nodded and continued down the path. Several minutes later they emerged out of the forest to an area covered in large boulders. Mike noticed that Marina carefully searched the area before she stepped out into the open.

He looked up into the rocks in the direction that Marina was staring. He blinked when a lean boy appeared a moment later followed by a slender young girl. From their coloring and build, he could see the resemblance to Marina.

Marina raised her hand and waved. "Come down. We must make camp before dark," she said.

Mike watched the two younger children carefully climb down. The boy turned several times to help the girl. Mike instinctively stepped forward and reached up to help the girl down from the last boulder. He didn't miss the look of fear that flashed through her eyes as they darted from him to Marina. He patiently waited for her to realize he meant no harm. Charlie helped by jumping up and putting his paws on the rock to reach eagerly for her hand with his long, wet tongue. The girl softly giggled when she felt Charlie's enthusiastic greeting.

"Come, Erin," Marina whispered reassuringly. "We must hurry."

Mike gently lowered the girl to the ground and turned in time to see Marina pause when the boy reached out to grip her arm. The boy's eyes were focused on Mike's face, and he could feel the barely contained animosity.

"Who is he?" Geoff demanded.

Mike didn't miss the slight movement of the boy's hand. Geoff's fingers were wrapped around the handle of a long knife sheathed at his waist. The look in his eyes must have warned the boy not to pull it out, because his hand wavered for a moment before falling to his side.

"I don't know, but he saved my life," Marina admitted in a quiet, hesitant voice.

The boy's eyes widened before his gaze moved back to Mike. "Which village are you from? You look different from us," Geoff said as a light of curiosity came into his eyes.

"No shit," Mike muttered before he flushed when Marina's lips twitched again. "I'm not from around here... Wherever, in the hell, 'here' is. Your name is Geoff, right?"

"Yes. I am Geoff, son of Ariness and Cornelia," Geoff stated. "What are you called?"

"Mike Hallbrook—Detective Mike Hallbrook and this fur-ball is Charlie. I work for the Lincoln County Sheriff's Department and the Yachats Police Department in Oregon. Listen, before I go any further, I want to know what is going on. What was that... thing back on the beach? Why are you hiding, and where are we going? I think before I go any further, I deserve some answers," he said, folding his arms across his chest.

He saw Marina's chin lift, and she gave him an impatient look before glancing up at the sky again. He could see the indecision on her face before she released the breath she was holding. There was a sense of apprehension in the stiffness of her shoulders as she gazed back at him.

"We do not have much time," she said, stepping closer to him until she was standing in front of him. "I am not sure what happened back on the beach. I cast a spell, and you appeared. You know this is my brother, Geoff, and this is my sister, Erin. I have told you who I am. The thing back on the beach was a creature summoned through black magic by the Sea Witch. She and her minions are who we hide from. We must seek safety before darkness descends."

"Why? Why before dark?" Mike asked in a soft tone.

Marina's expression grew sad before she turned her face away from him. "Because, the Sea Witch created a spell that drains our powers if we try to use them after dark. Without our magic, we would be defenseless against the creatures she created. Now, will you come with us or not? We cannot delay any longer," she explained quietly before looking up at him again.

Mike's lips tightened at the look of determination in Marina's eyes. He sensed that she was telling him the truth. Giving her a curt nod, he decided it was best to follow along, at least until he could figure out how to get back home. The last thing he wanted to do was meet up with more of those 'Hellhounds' in the middle of the night.

It was obvious he was no longer in Oregon. The question was—where was he? His gazed around at the growing darkness. Night when it should be mid-morning, the dead creature on the beach, Marina's talking magic bow, twin moons, and now a spell that drained magic—the list was growing.

Hell, with the way things are going, all I need to do is find a yellow brick road, change Charlie's name to Toto, and find a tornado to make this nightmare complete, he thought as he and Charlie followed behind the young girl called Erin.

CHAPTER SIX

Mike kept a keen eye on where they were going. They were heading in a different direction, away from the boulders and the beach. If the sun rose and set in the same directions as it did back home, then they were heading east.

He glanced at Marina. She was leading them along a winding, steep trail that ran parallel to a river. Nearly half a mile down the path, the river narrowed. He shook his head in wonder when she climbed the boulders up to a massive dead tree that created a bridge across the turbulent waters and the small waterfall created by the constriction of boulders and dead branches that had washed down the river.

Geoff turned and lifted Erin onto the tree, while Marina held out her bow to steady her sister and help pull her up. Charlie whined, not wanting to be away from the little girl who he had taken a shine to. It took a couple of tries, but with a little help from Geoff, the dog was able to scramble up onto the tree.

It was obvious from the silent teamwork that the three of them had worked together many times before in similar situations. Mike frowned when a strange and unexpected emotion swept through him as he studied Marina's expressive face. It felt like someone had reached inside him and tugged on his heart.

He didn't know if it was because he was confused by everything that had happened or if it was a phenomenon caused by being in this alternate reality. Whatever was causing the emotion, it was frustrating the hell out of him. Of course, he'd always been a sucker for a damsel in distress, even though this damsel could probably turn him into a toad if he wasn't careful.

Shaking his head, he climbed up after Geoff and navigated his way through the dried and broken limbs. Geoff swung around in front of Erin, calling for Charlie to follow him. Mike understood why when they reached the other side and had to work their way through the tangle of dried roots to the rocky shore of the river. Geoff helped Charlie down first before he turned back to help his younger sister. Once they were down, Geoff made a beeline for the forest. Mike looked up at the massive trees the size of the redwoods back home.

"Hurry," Marina softly called.

"Marina, I...," Erin started to say.

Mike reached out and steadied Erin when she slipped on the smooth river stones and almost fell. He motioned for Charlie to back up when the dog whined and pushed his nose against Erin's hand. Mike could feel heat radiating from Erin through the material covering her arms.

"Steady there. Marina, Erin feels like she has a fever," he said.

"Yes, I know. That is why we went to the village. She needs help. I had hoped the healer would help her more than she did, but it was too dangerous. We were lucky she helped us at all," Marina replied with a tired nod.

"Can't you make her better?" Mike asked, wrapping a supporting arm around Erin's waist before lifting her into his arms when her legs gave out. "I saw you do something to your leg back on the beach."

Marina shook her head and touched Erin's cheek with the tips of her fingers. "No, I can heal myself of minor wounds, but it does not work on others. I do not have the power to focus on their pain. With myself, I know what hurts and can focus enough to send a touch of healing to it. Erin has the gift to heal, but so many of the children have been ill lately that she is weak. Now, the sickness has found its way inside her," she murmured.

"Why didn't the healer help her more?" Mike asked with a frown.

"Because the Sea Witch would find out," Geoff answered bitterly, scratching Charlie's head when the dog circled around him. "We barely escaped as it was. The Sea Witch would have destroyed the village just as she destroyed ours."

"Sea Witch? You've mentioned her earlier. Who is she, and what do you mean by destroy the village?" Mike asked with a raised eyebrow. "Are you talking about a sea witch who lives at the bottom of the sea? Like in the story of the Little Mermaid?"

Erin giggled. "The mermaids do not like her," she whispered, resting her head against Mike's shoulder and closing her eyes. "The Sea King sent her to the bottom of the ocean. I wish she would have stayed there."

"He should have killed her when he had the chance! Isha said she tried to harm one of the Sea King's sons a year ago. Instead, he let her go again, and now she is here. We are almost to the tree where we will spend the night. Erin needs to rest, and she needs a chance to let the healing stones help her," Marina said before turning back and striding toward the woods.

"So, why did this Sea Witch come here? Can she live out of the water? I mean, isn't she like this octopus type creature or something?" Mike asked, shifting Erin in his arms.

Geoff snorted behind him. "Maybe the Sea Witch from your kingdom is," he said in a gruff tone. "She is the cousin of the Sea King. She can breathe on land or under the Sea, just like all the sea people can."

"She came to force our people to help her overthrow the Sea King. Papa said that she wanted to rule all of the Kingdoms. I don't know why, it seems like it would be most difficult," Erin whispered. Her eyes fluttered open, and she stared at Marina. "Tell him, Marina. Geoff is right. He might be the one Isha told us about."

"Who is this Isha, and tell me what?" Mike asked in frustration as they stepped between two large trees.

"Isha is our older brother," Marina explained.

"He was the King and Queen's Captain of the Guard," Geoff added, climbing over a tree trunk.

"Was?" Mike asked, carefully maneuvering over the log behind Geoff.

Geoff paused and looked at Mike. "The Sea Witch turned him, the Queen, and everyone in the palace to stone," he stated.

"Stone…." Mike repeated.

Erin shivered in his arms. "Everyone except the King. His heart and soul are frozen. Nothing can touch him, not even the Sea Witch," she whispered.

"Frozen…. Alrighty, I think I've definitely landed in an alternate reality," Mike muttered.

"We'll stay the night here. Charlie, Mr. Tree may not appreciate you watering him," Marina warned when the pup started sniffing the base of the tree.

Erin giggled again while Geoff snickered. Mike could totally understand Charlie's confused look. Marina had stopped in front of a tree that was twice as big as the others.

His arms tightened around Erin when she suddenly began to shiver uncontrollably. His skepticism must have shown on his face. Marina gave him a small smile before she reached forward and touched the trunk of the tree.

"Please, Mr. Tree, we need shelter for the night," she said.

Geoff's laugh warned Mike that his jaw was hanging down. He

snapped it shut, but that didn't keep the awe from his expression. The tree trembled under Marina's touch and the seam where the bark had healed opened to reveal a cavernous interior. Marina turned and motioned for them to go inside.

Mike bowed his head and followed Geoff and Charlie through the narrow opening. Straightening, he was surprised to see the interior was aglow with tiny green lights. Geoff shrugged off the pack he was carrying and set it on the ground. Mike turned in a tight circle. His gaze skimmed the interior. There was no way he was going to place Erin on the ground.

"I'll lay down a cover for Erin," Geoff said, reaching inside his pack.

"Let me have the fire sticks," Marina instructed.

Geoff looked up and scowled. "A fire won't last long. As soon as night falls completely, the fire will go out," he said.

"Yes, but at least it will give us some warmth," Marina retorted.

Mike looked up. The center of the tree was hollow all the way up. Near the top he could see places where small amounts of light shone. Looking back at Geoff, he waited for the boy to spread a thin blanket across the ground. He gently lowered Erin onto the blanket. Charlie immediately curled up next to the shivering little girl. Erin's thin arm wrapped around the pup.

Marina was pulling several short, fat sticks out of the bag. She stacked them in the center. Within seconds, they began to glow, and Mike could feel the heat. He was shocked when she adjusted one without it burning her.

She looked up at that moment and caught his surprised expression. Once again, the hint of a smile lifted the corner of her mouth. She stood up and picked up her bow.

"This will give us some warmth. Unfortunately, it won't last long. The magic will dissipate as the darkness of night grows," she explained with a hint of regret in her voice.

"Why don't you just build a regular fire?" Mike asked.

Marina briefly glanced at the opening before she turned back to him. He saw the regret and exhaustion in her eyes. His gaze moved to Geoff and Erin. The boy was pulling several more blankets out of the backpack. Mike watched him kneel next to his younger sister and cover her with one of them.

"It would take time to gather the wood. Even if we had wood, I have no flint with me," Marina said, walking over to kneel next to her sister.

"That is my fault. I should have been more attentive when I packed," Geoff said in a gruff voice.

Marina reached out and touched her brother's arm. She shook her head. There was a fierce, almost hard expression on her face.

"It was an accident. Accidents happen. Never blame yourself," she replied.

Mike could see the love for her brother on Marina's face. Whatever happened, it was obvious that the boy took the loss of the flint hard. In a situation like this, he could understand that sometimes a mistake or an accident could be the difference between life and death.

"I think I can handle this. You take care of your sister. I'll be back in a little while," Mike said.

Marina rose to her feet. Concern and a hint of panic swept across her face. She took a step closer to him, searching his face.

"Where are you going? It will be dark soon. Magna's spell will weaken you. You will be left defenseless," she said, shaking her head.

"You said that the spell drains magic, right?" Mike asked, lifting his hand to touch a strand of the mahogany hair that had come loose.

Confusion flickered through her eyes. "Yes," she answered.

Mike smiled. "I don't think I'll have to worry about her spell slowing me down. Your sister should be kept warm. Charlie is good, but even he can only do so much. Why don't you make her comfortable while I go get some firewood?" he suggested.

"But...."

Mike tenderly cupped Marina's jaw and gently laid his thumb across her lips. Bending forward, he paused a breath away from her lips. He wanted nothing more than to press his lips against hers and erase the look of fear in her eyes.

"I have my own magic, remember?" he reminded her.

Her head moved up and down in agreement. With a sigh of regret, Mike pulled away. He allowed his fingers the luxury of sliding along her jaw before he turned and disappeared through the opening, back out into the forest. Twilight had descended, and new sounds began to awaken.

"Remember your Boy Scout training, Mike," he said to himself as he began searching the ground for suitable firewood.

CHAPTER SEVEN

"Marina," Geoff said, pulling her out of the trance.

Marina turned to look at her brother. "Yes?" she asked.

"Do you...? Do you think he might be the one Isha said Mother talked about?" Geoff asked.

"I don't know… but, I hope so," she said, turning back to her brother. "Can you see if we have any food left in the bag? I'll place the healing stones around Erin."

"We have a little. I can make soup. That will make it stretch enough for all of us and be good for Erin," Geoff said.

Marina nodded, kneeling by her sister again. "Hurry before the fire sticks go out," she said.

Neither spoke as they worked. Geoff worked on making soup from the dried ingredients they had, and she focused on placing the healing stones on Erin. She had to reassure Charlie that she wasn't hurting her sister. The pup kept a keen eye on her as she worked.

Marina paused as she placed the last stone on the center of her sister's forehead. She could feel the heat radiating from Erin's skin before she even touched her. The feeling of helplessness rose up in her throat. What if the stones didn't work? What if Erin….?

"I'm going to go help Mike," Marina said, placing the last stone on Erin before rising to her feet.

"Darkness has come," Geoff warned, looking up at her in surprise.

Marina bent over and started to pick up her bow but decided to leave it. The bow wouldn't do her much good now. She swallowed back the bitterness threatening to choke her. Ignoring her fatigue, Marina focused on keeping herself upright, otherwise she would find herself back on the blanket beside Erin.

"I know. Try to finish the soup," she instructed.

"Be careful," Geoff called after her.

Marina gripped the bark of the tree and gave a sharp nod before continuing out into the darkness. She stumbled when the full weight of Magna's spell hit her. A shiver ran through her body, and she almost turned back. Instead, she gritted her teeth and pressed on. The fire sticks would burn for a short time longer than normal due to the protection of the tree, but even the tree could not protect them from the spell.

She stopped several feet outside of the tree and closed her eyes. Without her sense of sight, her hearing became sharper. She focused on each different sound. Tilting her head to the side, she turned to the left. The faint sound of rustling and the silence of the insects in that direction told her that someone or something was there.

Marina bit back a giggle when she heard a smothered curse. Opening her eyes, she headed in Mike's direction. He was only a few hundred feet from the large tree that was giving them shelter. In one arm, he held several long, thin branches. In his other arm, he had several decent size pieces of wood.

"Let me help you," Marina offered, stepping out of the shadows.

"Shit!" Mike exclaimed, dropping the bundles in his arms and reaching inside his jacket. He shook his head at her. "You need to call out a warning next time."

"I think half of the forest knows where you are," she chuckled.

"You have strange plants here. There was one that glows when you touch it," he commented.

"The Nightstars. They help light the forest. They are beautiful when they release their seeds once a year. The entire forest lights up," Marina explained.

She bent and pick up some of the dead limbs he had dropped. It wasn't until she straightened that the wave of fatigue hit her like a Tsunami, pulling the strength from her. Her lips parted on a cry of frustration when she felt the world begin to spin.

"Hey, steady there," Mike said, wrapping his arm around her waist.

"It's Magna's spell. I hate feeling so weak," Marina softly groaned.

"Why did you come out if you knew the spell would affect you like this?" Mike demanded, holding her close.

Marina leaned her head forward, resting her forehead against Mike's chest. She hadn't realized how tall or how broad he was. He also smelled incredibly good—warm with a hint of the rain-forest. A frown creased her brow as another feeling swept through her—she felt stronger—as if her magic flowed through her again.

Lifting her head, she gazed up at him with a puzzled frown. Her eyes searched his face. She couldn't see the aura of his magic, but he must have some to make her feel like this.

"What kind of magic do you have that can work against the power of the Sea Witch?" Marina asked with a faintly incredulous voice.

Mike's arm tightened around her, and he chuckled. "The good ole Hallbrook kind," he teased before his expression sobered, and he lifted a hand to brush it against her cheek. "Will you be okay?"

Marina nodded. "The nights are difficult, but with the first rays of the sun the spell lifts. We should get back to Erin and Geoff," she said.

She reluctantly pulled away from him. Almost immediately, she could feel a weight settle around her as Magna's spell drained her magic once again. Mike's arms fell away, and he studied her for several seconds before he bent over and picked up a stack of branches. He handed them to her when she held her arms out. He finished picking up the larger pieces and straightened.

Marina turned back toward the tree. She was confused by her reaction to Mike. When she touched him, she felt strong again—but there was something else. She also felt flustered. Her body reacted to him in a strange way. Just now, she had actually wanted to press her lips to his! The urge had never been so strong before. If that wasn't bad enough, she felt warm and tingly all over. For a moment, she wondered if she was coming down with the same sickness as the children.

Ducking her head, she stepped through the narrow opening in the tree. Geoff looked up in relief. She could see that the fire sticks were barely glowing. The small pot of soup had thin spirals of steam rising from it. Marina's gaze moved to Erin who was quietly lying with Charlie asleep by her side. Her sister's eyelids fluttered open.

"Are the healing stones helping?" Marina asked, placing the pile of branches down on the ground.

"They helped a little, but their magic faded with the sun. I'm so cold," Erin responded in a barely audible voice.

"Here," Mike said, setting down the limbs he'd been carrying next to the ones Marina had deposited.

Marina turned and watched as Mike shrugged off his jacket. He stepped forward and laid it over Erin. The stone she had placed on Erin's forehead slid off when her sister turned her head. Mike leaned down and picked up the stone. Marina gasped when she saw the sudden, powerful glow as he gently placed it back on Erin's forehead.

Erin must have felt the sudden influx of healing power because her body bowed upward. Mike's hand jerked back, and he straightened. Almost immediately, the glow faded, and Erin sank back against the blanket with a soft moan.

"Mike, touch the stone again," Marina said, stepping up to the blanket before sinking down next to her sister.

"What? I… What happened?" he asked, confused.

"I'm not sure. Please… touch the stone again," Marina begged.

She could see the hesitation on his face before he knelt down on one knee beside Erin. He reached out and gently touched the healing stone. Once again, it glowed with the magic held inside. Erin's eyes opened, and she stared up at Mike with wide eyes filled with awe.

"Now, move your fingers until you are touching Erin," Marina ordered.

He glanced at her before turning his gaze down to Erin's face. Sliding his fingers off the stone, he cupped the little girl's face with his large hand. Marina's lips parted when she saw the colorful aura of Erin's magic swirl around her sister. She hadn't seen it this strong in months!

Reaching out, she grasped Erin's right hand in hers. Marina closed her eyes when she felt the strength of her magic flowing through her. She opened her eyes and looked down at Erin.

Her sister's face was flushed, but not with the heat of fever. Instead, Marina could see the healthy glow on Erin skin. Several minutes later, Erin blinked. A wide smile lit the young girl's face.

"I'm hungry," Erin said, looking hopefully at Geoff.

Marina's throat tightened at the clear eyes and the smile that came naturally instead of being forced. She reached up and removed the healing stone from Erin's forehead and placed it on the blanket beside her sister. Erin sat up and bundled the blanket around her shoulders. Charlie softly groaned and shifted beside her, taking up the space Erin had made. Erin giggled and tenderly stroked the puppy.

"Thank you, Mr. Charlie, for keeping my spot warm," Erin teased.

Marina reached over and tenderly brushed the dark purple hair from Erin's cheek. The sound of her sister's teasing warmed Marina's heart. Even though she could feel the pull of Magna's magic on her, it wasn't enough to dampen her relief at seeing her sister feeling better.

"Warm soup coming up," Geoff said with a grin.

Turning her gaze back to Mike, she gave him a grateful smile. "Thank you," she said in a soft voice.

Mike shook his head. "I don't know what just happened, but whatever it was worked," he said, pushing up off the ground. "Let me make a fire. We don't want her to have a relapse."

Geoff removed the fire sticks that were no longer glowing and replaced them in his knapsack. Marina took the cup of soup from Geoff when he held it out to her. She bit her lip when she realized there was only enough for the three of them. Mike looked up and caught the expression of indecision on her face. Her blood heated when he gave her a slightly crooked grin.

"Eat. Charlie and I had a big breakfast a couple of hours ago," he said.

"I… If you are sure," Marina replied with a relieved smile.

He nodded and continued working on the fire. "What is this place called?" he asked.

"What do you mean? The forest? It is called Rindheart," Marina said.

Mike shook his head. "No, I mean this world. You called this place the Isle of Magic. Where exactly is it located? I come from a place called Earth and a town called Yachats in a state called Oregon and a country called the United States of America on the north American continent," he explained.

Marina thought about his question. "That is a lot of places to come from. This is the Seven Kingdoms. Our world is made up of seven isles, each a gift from the Goddess," she said.

"What is that?" Geoff asked when Mike pulled a small cylinder from his pocket and leaned closer to the stacked wood.

"Good old-fashioned magic called a cigarette lighter," Mike said, flicking the starter.

"How did it do that?" Geoff asked in excitement.

Mike chuckled. "I only have a basic idea, but it involves pressure, butane, air, and a catalytic coil. It is much easier than the Boy Scout method of rubbing two sticks together or using two flint rocks," he said.

"Do these Boy Scouts rule your world? You have mentioned them before," Marina asked in curiosity.

"No—It's kind of hard to explain. So, this is the Seven Kingdoms. It is sort of like our world where we have seven continents. Is each kingdom divided into different countries?" Mike asked, sitting back as the fire began to burn.

Geoff frowned in confusion. "What are countries?" he asked.

Mike raised an eyebrow. "I guess that is a no. So, each kingdom belongs to one species of people," he clarified.

"Yes," Erin said, smiling up at him. "We are the Isle of Magic. We each possess different kinds of magical abilities. Are you a healer as well? I felt stronger when you touched me."

Mike paused in breaking the long stick in his hand. Marina could see a flash of pain before he hid it. He shook his head and looked down at the fire.

"I wish, but no. I wouldn't say I have any magic abilities, but I'm good at what I do," he said.

"What are you good at?" Erin asked, licking a drop of soup from her bottom lip.

"Protecting people," he replied.

Warmth filled Marina when Mike looked at her. She looked away when Erin giggled and nudged her. A blush heated her cheeks. From under her lashes, she studied Mike as he asked questions and answered others from her brother and sister. She liked his patience with them and the sound of his smooth, rich voice.

Erin giggled when he teased her about the size of her yawn. Soon, the warmth of the fire Mike built, the stress of the day, and the drain on their magic was luring Marina and her siblings to sleep. Marina slid down next to Erin. Her sister was curled up next to Charlie and wrapped her arm around the pup. Marina lay with one arm curled under her head for a pillow.

"Here," Mike said, rising to his feet and covering both of them with another thin blanket and his jacket.

"What about you?" Marina asked.

"I'll be fine," Mike assured her, moving back to sit down again.

"Thank you," Marina replied before closing her eyes.

"Will you be here when we wake up?" Geoff asked, his exhaustion reflected in his voice.

Mike nodded. "Yes, I'll be here. Get some rest, I'll keep an eye on things," he said.

Geoff gave him a tired smile before pulling his blanket up to his neck and quickly falling asleep. Marina listened as Geoff and Erin's breathing slowed and became steady. She was too tired to open her eyes. The sound of the fire snapping, the warmth of her sister's body against her back, the heat of the fire in front of her, and the faint masculine scent clinging to Mike's jacket gave Marina a sense of security that she hadn't felt in over a year.

"Thank you," she murmured again.

"My pleasure, Marina. Get some sleep. I won't let anything happen to you guys," he replied in a soft voice.

CHAPTER EIGHT

Mike snapped some twigs and fed the fire. His gaze moved from the glowing worms that made their home in the tree to the woman sleeping across from him. He'd been trying not to stare at her but realized it was an impossible endeavor, especially in the cramped confines of their shelter.

"Marina Fae of the Isle of Magic. She's a witch, of course," Mike murmured under his breath. "A witch! A beautiful, exotic, daring, and brave witch."

He ran his gaze over her relaxed face. Wisps of her dark wavy hair caressed her cheek. Her coloring reminded him of the forest. Her dark brown and gold hair and tanned skin had the same highlights of the tree trunks with the sun shining on it. Her dark lashes lay like crescents against her sun-kissed cheeks. Her nose was long and slender while her lips made him want to taste their fullness.

Mike shook his head at his musing. *Since when have I ever been poetic?* he thought. *I really need to get my head examined. Instead of thinking of how much I want to kiss Marina, I should be focusing on what happened today, where I am, and how in the hell I'm going to get home!*

Silently rising to his feet, he decided he'd better collect more firewood. He motioned for Charlie to stay when the pup lifted his head. Turning, he quietly stepped around Geoff and slipped through the narrow opening in the trunk. He took several steps away before he paused and drew in a deep breath of the cool, clean air. He looked up at the night sky. One moon was full while the other looked like a waxing gibbous.

He kept the large tree to his right as he walked in a tight circle gathering several large pieces of dead wood. As he collected the wood, he listened to the different sounds of the forest. A hundred yards away, a large bird hooted from one of the tall trees. It sounded a lot like an owl. He could see the Nightstars light up and fade. The lights made the forest look more like something on a movie set or a theme park ride than a reality.

The sound of flapping wings and several dark shadows blocking the light from the moons drew Mike's attention to the treetops. Looking up, he caught his breath when he saw dozens of large birds flying overhead. At a rough guess, he'd have put their wingspan at almost twenty feet from tip to tip. He decided anything with wings that big must have an even larger beak. The last thing he wanted was to become their next meal.

He retraced his steps as silently as he could, wincing every time he stepped on a branch. Ducking his head, he entered the tree and released the breath he had unwittingly been holding. He quietly stacked the wood near the fire before taking two logs and placing them across the coals.

"I thought I had dreamed about you."

Mike's head jerked up, and his gaze locked with Marina's. She was watching him. He sank down to the ground next to Geoff.

"You should be sleeping," he chided.

"I know. It has been difficult to rest well over the past year. There is always a sense of fear that something will come for us in the dark, even though I know none of the Sea Witch's creatures can," she admitted.

"Why can't she attack at night?" Mike asked with a frown.

Marina drew in a deep breath and released it. "She created a spell that drains all magical creatures of their powers from nightfall to dawn. You would think she would have realized that the same spell would affect her and the creatures she made, but for some reason she didn't. She—and the unnatural beasts she uses like the ogres—are just as defenseless as the rest of us. Unfortunately, there are still things that can hurt us," she explained.

"Well, that was a big uh-oh," Mike chuckled, poking at the fire with a stick.

"Yes, but at least her mistake gives us some reprieve," Marina replied with a yawn.

"Get some sleep. We should have enough firewood to last until morning," he assured her.

"What about you?" she asked, biting her lip.

Mike smiled and shook his head. "It is still morning for me. You don't have to worry about me too. I'm old enough to take care of myself," he responded.

Her lips twitched at his comment. "Yes, you are," she murmured on a yawn. "You are a very…."

Mike stopped poking the fire and waited for her to finish the sentence. He was a very… what? A silent groan echoed through his head when he realized that she had fallen back asleep. It took him a moment to realize he was still staring at her—and that his body was hard and throbbing.

Leaning back against the inside of the tree, Mike blinked. What the fuck was going on? His body hadn't reacted to a woman like this since he was about fourteen and Kylie Mooney sat in front of him in eighth grade science.

He itched to bury his fingers in her long hair, but it was his cock that he wanted to bury somewhere else. He tilted his head back and watched the wisps of smoke rise from the fire to the top of the tree. It was going to be a long, long night.

"Come on, boy. You've watered enough trees," Mike called to Charlie.

Beside him, Mike heard Geoff chuckle. The teen had become his shadow since he and his sisters woke up as the sun peaked over the horizon. Mike wasn't sure if it was because the boy wanted to know more about him or if it was to keep an eye on him. When Mike stated he needed to take Charlie out for a bit, Geoff had eagerly stood up as well.

Mike shoved his hands into the pockets of his jacket. He had wanted to go with Marina when she said she would find some food to break their fast but, before he could suggest it, she had disappeared. Erin stayed to pack up their blankets.

"He listens well," Geoff commented when Charlie came up.

"When he feels like it," Mike retorted with a wry grin.

Mike watched as Charlie came trotting toward them with a long stick that kept getting caught in the tall ferns. Of course, Charlie didn't come to Mike. Geoff bent over and gave Charlie a rub when the pup dropped the stick at the boy's feet.

"Watch him. He's playing you. If you try to grab the stick, he'll take off," Mike warned.

Geoff grinned and winked at Mike. One second Geoff was there, and in the next he was gone. Mike stumbled backwards and blinked—and blinked again, and again. Either he was having issues with double vision or there were now two Golden Retrievers.

Mike lifted a hand and rubbed it over his eyes. Looking between his fingers, he still saw two dogs. They looked identical.

"Geoff, knock it off," Marina ordered, walking past them.

Mike started and turned to look at her. She was carrying several large, dark orange roots by their leaves. In a flash, Geoff was back into the shape of a teen and following her back to the tree. Mike looked down when Charlie whined. He could see the pup's gaze following Geoff.

"I've fallen down the fucking Rabbit's hole!" he muttered before shaking his head. "Come on, boy."

Marina scowled at her brother. Geoff just grinned at her, adding to her irritation. Bending over, she grabbed the pot and held it out to him.

"I need water," she stated, staring at him with a raised eyebrow.

"What's wrong?" Geoff asked with a grimace, taking the pot from her.

Marina opened her mouth to scold her brother for startling Mike. She snapped her mouth closed and pursed her lips when Charlie entered their shelter a moment before Mike did. Turning, she knelt by the hot coals leftover from the fire and pulled her knife out.

"Charlie!" Erin called, opening her arms wide.

The pup didn't need any other encouragement. His furry, wiggling body almost knocked Marina over in his haste to get to her sister. Fire swept through Marina when she felt a pair of strong hands steady her.

"Sorry about that," Mike said, kneeling down next to her. "He still needs to learn some manners."

"So does my brother," Marina retorted before she blew out a breath and turned her head to look at Mike. She was startled to see his face so close to hers. "He… he shouldn't have startled you."

Her eyes widened when he lifted his hand and brushed her hair back from her cheek. His fingers caressed her earlobe as he tucked the long, thick strands behind her ear. Marina leaned closer to his body when his fingers traced the line of her jaw.

"It was actually pretty cool—unexpected, but cool. Can you…?" Mike asked in a slightly hesitant voice.

Marina shook her head. "We each have our own strengths and weaknesses. I have an affinity for the forest—and…." She paused and shook her head again. "Geoff can imitate living creatures. It is forever getting him in trouble. If he is not careful, a hunter or meat-eating animal will mistake him for their next meal," she said in exasperation.

"So, Erin can heal, Geoff can imitate living things, and you can…," Mike encouraged, turning to sit down on the ground so he was facing her.

"Marina can talk to the trees and plants," a voice replied.

Marina grimaced when Mike jerked his head around to look at the bow that was propped up against a log. Erin giggled at his reaction while Charlie stood up and walked over to sniff the bow. Mike chuckled when the bow growled at Charlie. The pup yelped and hurried back to lay next to Erin.

"Is that thing for real?" Mike asked, studying the bow.

A reluctant grin curved Marina's lips at the sound of awe in his voice. She glanced at her bow before focusing on cutting up the roots she brought back for their breakfast. Once boiled, it would make a thick, creamy, and delicious meal that was high in protein and nutrients.

"My father gave Mr. Bow to me when I turned eight summers old. The wood came from an ancient elder tree. They are the oldest trees on the Isle of Magic. It is said that the elder trees were planted by the Goddess herself and contain the elements of magic that give us our power. The forest is protected by a magic so old that not even the Sea Witch's evil can touch it. Father was given the gift of a limb after he healed a sick tree. My gift of magic comes from him while Erin's comes from our mother. We like to tease Geoff and say he was a foundling, because no one knows where his gift came from," Marina said, looking up when Geoff entered with the pot of water.

"That is not true. Our grandmother is a shapeshifter. Here is the water," Geoff said, placing the pot of cold water on the bed of coals from the fire.

"Thank you," Marina replied, adding the roots to the water.

"Erin, do you want to take Charlie out for a walk?" Geoff asked with a hopeful look at his younger sister.

"Yes," Erin answered, rising to her feet. "Come on, Charlie."

Marina looked up with a worried frown. "Don't go far, and keep your eyes open," she cautioned.

"We will," Geoff promised.

She bit her lip and watched as they slipped through the opening. Both of them were aware of the dangers, but she couldn't help but worry after yesterday. Erin looked better this morning, but she was still pale and far too thin for her age.

Her sister had lost weight over the last couple of months. The strain of caring for so many children who had fallen ill, then becoming sick herself had left Erin with little appetite. When they returned to the camp later today, she would place the healing stones around Erin again.

"What is that?" Mike asked with a sniff.

Marina blinked and turned to look at Mike. She parted her lips as she stared at his mouth. She wondered what his lips would feel like against hers. He must have read her expression because he leaned forward and cupped her cheek with his hand. She lifted her eyelashes and became captivated by the burning expression in his eyes.

"Mike…," Marina murmured, leaning toward him.

A soft moan escaped her when his lips captured hers. She raised her arms and wrapped them around his neck when he slid his hands around her waist and lifted her enough to pull her onto his lap. She threaded her fingers through his short hair, holding him to her.

Their hot breaths mixed as their tongues tangled with each other, each seeking to satisfy the hunger that had been ignited. Marina felt the magic inside her soar to a level she had never experienced before. Her body trembled with need for the man who had saved her life and connected with her on an elemental level.

"Woof!"

The sound of Charlie's bark pulled Marina back to reality. She reluctantly broke their kiss, her eyes still closed as she clung to the wave of emotion still washing over her. Eyelashes fluttering, she looked up when she felt Mike stiffen and heard his swiftly inhaled breath.

Her dazed gaze met his. His hand slid from her waist to tenderly touch her cheek. His fingers skimmed along her flushed, heated skin. In the reflection of his eyes, she could see the glow surrounding her.

"I'm not sure what is happening, but I can promise you, I intend to see where it takes us," he stated in a determined voice.

Marina flushed with pleasure and released him. Her body was glowing—literally. She held her hands out in front of her and turned them. Looking up, her lips parted. She could see the awe reflected in his gaze. He could see her aura.

"Marina, is the food ready? I'm starving," Erin called.

Marina slid off of Mike's lap and knelt in front of the fire again as Charlie, followed closely by Erin and Geoff, entered their small shelter. She quickly picked up the spoon and stirred the root mush she had been cooking. Luckily, it didn't stick to the bottom of the pot or burn.

"It is almost ready," Marina said.

Erin paused as she started to sit and stared at her. Marina could feel her cheeks heating and had to resist the urge to lick her lips. Erin sank down the rest of the way and tilted her head.

"Are you feeling well? You look flushed," Erin asked in concern.

"I'm fine. Here, we need to eat and leave. We still have a long way to go before we get back to camp," Marina said, holding out a bowl of mush to Erin.

CHAPTER NINE

Less than an hour later, Mike was following Marina as they navigated a narrow mountain trail. On one side was a wall of rock while on the other was a steep, tree covered drop off. This time, Geoff led the way with Charlie, Erin, Marina, and Mike following single file behind him.

For the first time, Mike noticed that while Marina's top looked black, it was actually a forest green that changed colors in the sunlight. The colors helped her blend in with the surrounding forest. He swore that at times, she actually appeared to fade from view.

He had to admit that he was fascinated with everything about this woman walking in front of him. Their shared kiss earlier this morning kept playing like a broken record over and over in his mind. The taste of her lips, the feel of her warm body against his, the passion in her response—hell, even his own reaction!

He wanted her. There was no denying it, and he wasn't even going to try. When she had pulled back after hearing Charlie's bark, her skin had been glowing. The vivid rainbow of colors had wrapped around his hand when he touched her. There had been a tingling feeling, almost as if he had touched one of those plasma balls that he used to play with as a kid.

He wanted to know more about her, and he wanted to protect her. Watching her sleep last night had awakened a strong, protective instinct inside that had startled him. He hadn't felt such a strong reaction for anyone before, not even for Ruth. Of course, he'd never had to worry about an evil Sea Witch, Hellhounds, ogres, magical realms, or things like that with his sister, just a wimpy ex-husband.

A shudder went through him at the thought of his sister. He had to find a way back. If he didn't, there was no doubt in his mind that Ruth would turn Yachats State Park upside down trying to find him. If there was one thing his sister was—it was tenacious. She could be worse than Charlie with a chew bone!

"We are almost there," Marina commented over her shoulder, pulling him back to the present.

"Sounds good," Mike replied.

Nearly fifteen minutes later, the path curved downward and opened to reveal a wide, flat area near the base of the mountain. Mike paused when he saw the makeshift shelters. There were a half-dozen small campfires burning outside of the branch-and-woven-leaf structures. Dozens of children of all ages paused to look at them in fear for a brief moment before a cry of relief and excitement resounded from the group.

Mike quickly found himself surrounded by a sea of dirty, tired faces looking up at him in curiosity, reserve, and a touch of hope. He turned his head and locked gazes with Marina as she reached out and gently touched several of the rumpled children. A combination of love, sadness, and determination was reflected in her expression.

"Who are they? Why are they here?" he asked. A dark, puzzled frown creased his brow when he didn't see anyone older than Marina. "Where are the adults?"

"Gone," Marina quietly replied as she gazed around the suddenly quiet group. "Their parents and many of their siblings and friends were turned to stone by the Sea Witch for refusing to join her. The few villages that survived are those who pay tribute to Magna, hoping to save themselves. The children you see here were the only ones lucky enough to escape into the forest before the spell consuming their villages could affect them."

Mike's eyes widened as the large scale devastation of what had happened to Marina's people hit him. He was in a strange world, among a tide of mahogany and violet-haired urchins whose parents had been turned to stone by a Sea Witch straight out of a fairy tale. He swallowed as he watched Charlie eagerly moving from one small body to the next, licking them and eating up the attention. He returned his gaze to Marina when she gently touched his arm.

"Come, I need to check on a few things. I also want to make sure that I place the healing stones on Erin for a little while. Before sunset, I will prepare some food for us. I know a place where we can talk in private," she said in a quiet voice.

Mike nodded. "What can I do to help?" he asked as he followed her.

A grateful smile lit her features. "If you could help Geoff check the shelters, I would appreciate it. The children were building them when we left a few days ago," she said.

Mike glanced around the small encampment and nodded. "I can do that," he responded.

He turned back to look at Marina when she touched his arm. He saw a flash of uncertainty on her face before she drew in a deep breath, leaned forward and brushed a kiss against his cheek. He wrapped his arms around her waist, pulling her tight against him.

"Mike!" Marina gasped in surprise, looking up at him.

"That is not a kiss." He lowered his head until he was a breath away from her lips. "Now… this *is* a kiss," he murmured.

He captured her parted lips. There was no doubt in his mind that he wanted this woman with a passion that nearly took his breath away.

The chemistry between them immediately ignited a fire inside him, and the mischievous kiss he'd planned soon turned into a forget-the-world, this-woman-is-mine kind of kiss. He raised a hand and tangled his fingers in her hair so he could deepen the kiss.

Mike literally forgot about everything but the soft, warm woman in his arms. At least, he did until he felt a tug on his pant leg. Breaking the kiss with an impatient growl, he turned his head to see what had disturbed him.

His expression cleared when he saw a young girl who must have been no more than three staring up at him with wide eyes of crystal blue. Her cheeks had streaks of dirt on them, and her ice-blue curly hair was in a lopsided ponytail. Mike heard Marina's soft groan.

"Kacie, where's your brother?" Marina asked.

"Touch!" Kacie demanded, still staring at Mike.

Mike grimaced at the piercing gaze. "Why is she staring at me?" he asked.

"She is trying to read you. Kacie is an Empath," Marina explained.

"An Empath...," Mike shook his head. "I don't think it would be a good idea for her to read me at the moment."

Marina turned to look at him with a frown. "Why?" she asked.

"Because what I'm thinking and feeling is definitely for mature audiences only," he ruefully admitted.

"I don't...," Marina began before understanding dawned. Her face turned a rosy red. "Oh!"

"Yeah, that about sums it up," he chuckled.

"Kacie! Kacie, where are you?" a young boy called from outside one of the shelters.

Mike could see the boy frantically searching for the little girl. Marina bent over and picked up Kacie. The boy turned toward them when he saw his sister. Mike could see the boy's exasperated expression. A grin curved his lips—Ruth had worn the same expression more than once with him.

"I'll go find Geoff," Mike said.

"I think Kacie and I will go check on Erin," Marina replied before turning back toward him. "I will see you later?"

Mike could hear the slight hesitation in her voice. "You bet your ass you will," he retorted with a wink.

Turning, he headed across the encampment to the shelter Geoff was working on. He needed something to keep his mind occupied—well, at least partially occupied if for no other reason than to get his body back under control. At the moment, his cock was still hard, and he could feel the sexual desire still pulling at him.

"This is nothing like being fourteen—this is far, far worse. I'll be heading into some serious trouble if I'm not careful," he muttered under his breath.

~

Marina bit her lip as she watched Mike working with Geoff. The day had warmed up, and he had removed his jacket and sweater. The black short-sleeve shirt he'd worn under his sweater clung to his body, highlighting his broad chest and flat stomach.

A light blush heated her cheeks when Mike turned his head as if feeling her gaze and caught her staring at him. She whispered to one of the other young girls who had come to sit with Erin while Marina helped prepare food for the younger children.

"You like him," Erin observed.

Marina flushed and pursed her lips together when several of the other girls giggled. She drew in a breath, released a loud sigh, and scowled at the other girls who were now watching her. Her gaze moved back to

Mike where he was tying off a section of the wall he and Geoff had constructed.

"He's not from our world," Marina murmured, turning her attention back to stirring the wild vegetables two of the other girls had gathered, cleaned, and cut up.

"Why should that matter? Father always said that he would love Mother, even if she came from the Isle of the Monsters," Erin replied with a raised eyebrow.

Marina chuckled. "Mike is not from any of the kingdoms in our world. It is only natural that he will want to return to where he came from," she explained.

"Then, what kingdom does he come from?" Chai, a young girl the same age as Geoff, asked.

"He came from a strange place with many names that I have never heard," Marina admitted.

"Could we go to his world? Would we be safe there?" Dara asked.

Marina's gaze softened at the young girl's hopeful look. She shook her head. Even if she knew how she had opened the door in the first place, she seriously doubted she could do it again.

Handing the spoon she had been using to stir the large pot of soup to Chai, Marina stood up and crossed over to where her sister was sitting. She ran her hand over Erin's forehead. She breathed a sigh of relief when it felt cool to her touch—the healing stones had done their magic.

"Marina… What are we going to do?" Erin asked.

"I don't know, but I'll think of something," she replied.

She paused, her hand still against Erin's cheek. The other girls had stopped what they were doing to look at her. She could see the exhaustion on all of their faces. Looking around the camp, she could not only see it on the other children's faces, but feel it in the air. The constant moving, the lack of regular food, the sickness that had swept through the small group, and the perpetual fear of being found was taking a toll on everyone.

Once their new camp was finished, she would leave Geoff in charge of the group and seek help from the one person who might understand how she had opened the portal between her world and Mike's. She would also ask for help in reaching out to the other kingdoms. Despair filled her at the thought that the other kingdoms would turn her away.

"Marina! We finished the last shelter," Geoff said with an easy smile.

Marina removed her hand from Erin's cheek. A laugh escaped her when Charlie came up and licked her sister's cheek. Of course, the pup —excited by all of the girls' reactions—had to give each one a lick. The squeal of laughter was music to her ears. It had been so long since she'd heard the happy sound that she'd often wondered if she would ever hear it again.

"It looks like Charlie has found some willing victims to love on," Mike chuckled.

Marina started in surprise. She was so focused on Charlie's antics that she didn't hear Mike's approach. Twirling, she found herself in his arms once again. Lifting her head, she drew in a deep breath when she saw the fire burning in his eyes.

"I… Yes, he has," she said in a slightly breathless voice.

"Do you need help with anything else?" Mike asked.

The giggles behind Marina told her that the girls knew exactly what was going on—well, at least the older ones. Even Geoff was looking at her funny. With a slight growl of annoyance, Marina glared at the children watching and listening to them so intently. Of course, all that did was make them giggle harder.

"Mr. Bow, let's go fishing," Marina called.

In a flash, the bow flew through the air to her outstretched hand. Turning, she tossed her long braid over her shoulder. She had only taken a few steps before she stopped in her tracks.

"Would you… Would you like to help me catch some fish for dinner?" she asked, looking at Mike over her shoulder.

"Of course I'd love to help you! What kind of man turns down the offer of a fishing trip with a beautiful witch?" he teased.

"A smart one if he doesn't want to have to clean the wiggling, disgusting things," Mr. Bow retorted.

A surprised look appeared on Mike's face before he burst out in a deep, rich laugh that sent a wave of need through Marina. How could a man's laugh make her want to strip him out of his clothing and do wild things to him? She softly groaned when she heard the laughter of the children again. Focusing on where she was going, she strode across the encampment toward a path that led down to the river.

"Marina," Mike said, following her down the winding path. "Marina, wait."

Marina stopped. She held her back stiff and her head high. Turning on her heel, she faced Mike. Confusion, frustration, and another emotion she didn't understand warred inside her.

"What is it?" she demanded.

Mike drew to a stop in front of her. Lifting his hand, he gently pulled free a long piece of straw that had become tangled in her hair. He held it up, twirling it between his fingers.

"This…," he said before bending down to brush a kiss across her lips. "And that."

Her eyelids lowered to conceal her confusion. Once again, she felt a need rising inside her—a need to touch him, to kiss him, and to be close with him in a way she had never been with a man before. Her magic reached out to wrap around him. She could see the spirals of her aura curling outward.

"Mike...."

Her voice faded. She honestly didn't know what to say to him. How did she explain the rush of emotions filling her whenever she thought of him when she didn't understand them herself?

"I know, Marina. I feel it too," he said, cupping her cheek and bending down to brush another kiss across her lips.

"Fishing—that is what we are supposed to be doing, correct? Or were you planning on using Mike's worm instead?" Mr. Bow dryly commented.

A wave of embarrassment swept through Marina, and she lifted her bow and shook it. "I should use you as firewood," she threatened, holding up her bow so she could glare at it. "How Mother ever allowed Father to give you to me is beyond rational thought. You are completely incorrigible!"

"My personality comes naturally, of course. All elder trees are born with a dry sense of humor," Mr. Bow retorted.

"I'm so sorry," Marina said with an apologetic grimace to Mike. "I really have no control over what Mr. Bow says."

Mike chuckled. "I can imagine having Mr. Bow can make life very interesting at times," he replied, stepping next to her and threading his fingers through her hand.

"You have no idea," she mumbled.

A shiver ran through her when he lifted her hand and pressed a kiss to the back of it. She briefly closed her eyes and drew in a deep breath. For just a little while, she wanted to forget everything else but them.

"Fishing, Marina. It will be dark soon," Mr. Bow reminded her.

"I know, Mr. Bow," Marina reluctantly said, releasing the breath in a sigh and pulling back from Mike.

CHAPTER TEN

The river was shallow along the edges before gradually deepening in the center. Large boulders, washed down from the mountain over time, created small, still pools. The water was crystal clear here, which made it easier to see the fish that liked to school in calmer waters.

They worked in silence. Mike watched in amazement as Marina stood on one of the boulders and pulled the bowstring back. A glowing arrow appeared. She held steady—watching and waiting—before she released the bowstring.

Mike decided that it would have been magical just to watch Marina without Mr. Bow. A golden string was attached to the arrow, and she would pull in the fish and toss it to him. Using the knife Geoff had given him earlier, Mike cleaned the fish, filleting and placing them in woven baskets of vines that Marina had created. Each fish was almost twice the size of the Wild Alaskan Salmon he used to catch in Alaska, and they quickly filled two large woven baskets.

He had finished up the last one when an unusual sound caused him to look up. He froze with his hand in midair. Across the river stood a huge, hairy creature that looked like a cross between a miniature King

Kong and a water buffalo. Shaggy, dark-brown and black hair covered its body. From the neck down, it looked and walked like an ape. It had a long snout and horns that curved along its skull, which looped around on either side, ending in sharp points.

The beast raised its head and sniffed the air. A feeling of unease swept through Mike when the creature lowered its head and stared at him. Drawing in a deep breath, he kept his gaze on the creature.

"Marina… We've got company," he softly called.

"I know," she replied.

Mike's gaze flashed to Marina where she stood on the boulder, grinning. He turned back to stare at the creature that was now wading through the water. Mike took an instinctive step backwards when it reached the middle of the river.

"I don't know if I should freeze, run like hell, or pinch myself," he said.

Marina's laughter filled the air. It was warm, sexy, and made him think of all kinds of things, which he shouldn't be at the moment. From the corner of his eye, he watched her squat and slide down off the boulder. She walked to the edge of the water and waited.

"Come here, my friend," Marina murmured, lifting her right hand.

Mike watched in disbelief as it finished crossing the river and slowly waded up to the rocky edge. The water ape, as he decided to call it for lack of a better name, stopped and lowered its head to Marina's hand. It sniffed her palm before licking it.

"What's it doing?" Mike asked in a curious voice.

Marina looked at him over her shoulder and smiled. "The River Beasts love fish. They are normally solitary creatures and usually only come down from the trees to feed. This one must have been close by and smelled the fish you were cleaning," she explained.

"Oh… Kind of like an overgrown koala, only—not," he replied.

"I don't know what this koala is, but they are normally very gentle creatures for their size," she said, scratching the River Beast's forehead. "Could you bring the remains of one of the fish to me please?"

Mike gingerly bent down and picked up one of the discarded remains of a fish. He straightened and slowly walked toward the River Beast. The animal had a head the size of a semi cab and stood close to twenty feet high. Holding the fish out, he was surprised when the creature reached out with one hand and pinched the tail between its finger and thumb.

He released the fish when the River Beast lifted it up. The creature paused to gaze down at him for a moment before it tilted its head back and opened its mouth. The carcass of the fish disappeared in one bite. Mike stumbled to the side when the River Beast slowly moved past him toward the pile of fish remains.

"Hey, don't…," Mike started to protest when the beast paused by one of the baskets.

"It's alright. He won't take the fish in the basket. He knows we need them," she murmured.

He turned his head when he felt Marina touch his arm. She gave him an encouraging smile before nodding toward the beast. Sure enough, the creature turned its head back to the pile of remains. The ground shook slightly when the River Beast suddenly sat down on its haunches. Reaching out, the creature slowly began eating the fish carcasses one at a time.

"It has been tough on them since the Sea Witch created her Hell-hounds. Over the past year, I have found the remains of three River Beasts," Marina said in a sad voice before she shook her head and looked up at the sky. "It will be dark in little over an hour. We better get back to the encampment."

Mike nodded. He watched as Marina walked over to the creature. She gently stroked the River Beast before murmuring something to it. A smile lifted the corner of his mouth when the creature snorted and picked up the last fish. He stepped to the side when it walked by him, heading once again for the river. He followed the creature's departure until it disappeared into the forest on the other side.

Turning, Mike noticed that Marina had picked up one of the baskets and was waiting for him. He walked over and picked up the other one. They walked back up the path to the village in silence, each lost in their own thoughts once again.

Nearly an hour later, the smell of fresh grilled fish and rich soup filled the air around the village along with the happy sighs of sated children. Marina was impressed that Mike helped her and the older children in preparing plates for the younger children first. Only when everyone else had finished eating and begun to settle down did Marina and Mike prepare a meal for themselves.

With an uncertain smile, Marina motioned for Mike to follow her as she stepped out of the hut. Out of habit, her eyes scanned the area to make sure everything was as it should be. The older children were cleaning up and softly talking while the younger ones were already beginning to settle down for the night. The weight of the Sea Witch's spell drained the energy of the youngest children more quickly than the older ones.

Marina could feel the spell pulling on her own body. For a brief moment, her gaze met that of her brother. He was lying near one of the outdoor fires with Charlie curled against his side. Geoff gave her a worried look. She smiled in reassurance. She knew he was still worried about Erin. Satisfied, he laid his head back down.

"There is a place not far from here that I like to go in the evenings. It is close enough to the encampment that I can hear if anyone needs me but far enough that we can talk in private," Marina murmured.

He inclined his head, letting her know that he heard her. Marina wove her way through the small encampment and headed toward a path that cut through the rocks on the opposite side from the other path that led down to the river. They both walked in silence until they emerged through a narrow gap onto a wide ledge that looked down over the island. From this vantage point, a person could see almost all of it.

"Wow!" Mike exclaimed in a hushed voice. "This is… incredible."

Marina chuckled and motioned for him to sit beside her as she sat down on a flat rock. There was a light breeze, and she lifted her head to draw in a deep breath of the fresh air. Despite her exhaustion, she couldn't help but appreciate the beauty of her home.

"Try one of these," she suggested in a quiet voice, nodding to a large green seed. "The liquid inside is very refreshing and good for the body."

Mike picked up one of the green pods. He studied it for a moment before taking a bite. She smiled when his eyes widened in surprise before he devoured the nutritious pod.

"This is delicious!" he exclaimed, reaching for another one.

"They are and thankfully plentiful if you know where to look," she replied.

Marina balanced her plate on her lap. From where they sat, they had a perfect view of the valley and the coastline. They ate in silence, watching as the twin moons rose and illuminated the valley far below. Along the coast, the waves breaking against the rocky shore and the sparkle of bioluminescence algae made the water look like it was a river of blue stars.

"Tell me about your world, Mike," Marina quietly encouraged, not looking at him but staring out over the valley. "What is it like? What… is your life like there?"

"It's different," Mike admitted. He turned so he was facing the unusual woman sitting next to him. "The things you talk about belong in fairy tales in my world. I'm a detective for the Lincoln County Sheriff's Office. I was investigating the disappearance of two women that vanished in the past two years…."

Marina turned to look at him when his voice faded. She studied the wave of expressions that crossed his face as he looked down at the plate in his hands. A dark frown creased his brow. He placed his empty plate down on the rock next to him and stood up to walk over to the ledge. Marina placed her plate on top of his and stood up. She silently walked over to stand next to him. He was staring out across the Isle of Magic.

"What is it?" she asked, tilting her head.

In the distance, she could barely make out the towers that were part of the palace. They rose high above the trees like a shadowy hand reaching for the moons. A shiver ran through her, and she wrapped her arms around her waist. So much joy had once belonged there. Now, only sorrow and evil lived within the once magnificent stone walls.

"I wonder...," he whispered, his voice faint as if he were deep in thought. "I wonder if they found a way to your world."

"Who found a way?" Marina asked, confused.

"The two women I was investigating...," he replied, his voice fading again.

"There have been no strange women here. If there had been, Isha would have told Father and Mother. Word of such an event would have spread quickly," she said, biting her lip and frowning. "But... Isha did mention something."

He turned to face her. He reached out and gripped her arms in a light but firm hold. Immediately, she could feel the burst of energy rush through her. The force of it was so powerful that for a moment it took her breath away, and she forgot what they were talking about.

"She mentioned...," he asked when her voice faded.

She looked up at him. "I heard Isha talking to Father and Mother about how Drago, the Dragon King, had awoken. It must have been about two years ago. Isha said that the Queen believed good things would happen. The dragons were magnificent to behold and none were more powerful than Drago. I was not much older than Erin when Drago disappeared. It is said that he was so grief stricken by the loss of all his people, that the Isle of the Dragons disappeared into a mist of sorrow. There were only two things that Father said could awaken the Dragon King—one was the return of his people, and the second was someone trying to steal from the dragon's treasure." A bemused smile curved her lips. "Isha said a strange female had stolen something of extreme value; she had stolen Drago's heart. Isha told Father that the King and Queen sent a gift of peace and congratulations.... And shortly before the Sea Witch took over the Isle of Magic, I was talking with a friend of mine from the Isle of the Sea Serpent. Karin told me that the Sea King had taken a bride who stood up to the Sea Witch—a strange female from another world with hair the color of fire coral."

"Hair the color of fire coral.... She had to be talking about Jenny Ackerly," Mike whispered, staring down at her in amazement. "It has to be them. Carly Tate had a thing for dragons. Everyone I interviewed talked about her obsession with them. Jenny Ackerly has red hair. They must have found a way to this world somehow."

"You mean, the women came from your world as well?" Marina asked, her lips parting as hope began to flare inside her. "If they did, perhaps if you talked to them, they would talk to their mates. They could convince Drago and the Sea King to help us! The power of both the King of the Dragons and the Sea King would surely be too much for the Sea Witch. Mike, you have to talk to them. You have to ask them for their help," she begged, clutching his arms. "Please... for my people, for my parents, and the villagers... and the children. You have to help us."

CHAPTER ELEVEN

Marina's plea for help deeply touched him. The discontented feelings with his life that he'd been wrestling with for the past few years had disappeared since he first saw her. Hell, discontent was one word he wouldn't associate with Marina. His body came alive when he touched her, making him feel energized! Even the strange colors that swirled around her were now flowing around him as if they were melting at his touch.

His left hand moved up her arm, as if it had a mind of its own, to thread through the thick braid at her neck. He splayed his fingers against her smooth, pale skin. He heard her slight, quick gasp of breath as he captured her softly parted lips with his own.

Once again, the moment their lips connected he felt the familiar explosion deep inside his gut that spread outward, slowly engulfing him in the fiery whips of its flames. He closed his eyes and swore he could see a brilliant burst of light as if a star had just exploded and opened up before him, spiraling outward in a mass of colorful gases forming the galaxies. The intensity behind this kiss was beyond their growing physical attraction. It was as if the silver threads that made up the fabric of the universe were weaving around them and piecing two halves of a soul together as one.

So this is what magic feels like, he thought in a daze as a jolt of energy poured through him in one explosive burst after another.

He groaned when Marina's lips parted under his, sending a shattering wave of fire through him. A shudder ran through him when she tentatively touched the tip of her tongue to his bottom lip. His body reacted like a school boy getting his first kiss behind the bleachers—only magnified a thousand times.

Marina moaned softly when he slid his other hand down her arm and around her waist to pull her closer. Sliding the hand gripping her neck around to her jaw, he tenderly caressed the strong line as he deepened the kiss. He knew he wasn't going to last long when one of Marina's hands slid down his chest and the other wrapped around his neck to hold him against her. A shudder ran through him when her hand slipped under the hem of his shirt to his heated flesh. Breaking the kiss, he rested his forehead against hers and drew in a deep breath.

"This is crazy. If we don't stop, I will be taking you right here and now," he muttered, closing his eyes for a moment as he fought to control his raging desire. He opened his eyes and he drew back. Marina's glazed expression told him that she was experiencing the same intense reaction that he had felt. "What the hell just happened? I mean… I know what happened, but… What the hell happened?"

A soft chuckle escaped Marina as she stared up into his stunned eyes. "It is said that when a witch touches the one destined to be her mate, the universe opens to them for a moment so they can see all the wonders held within it, and they would understand where her powers came from," she whispered. "I saw it. Did you?"

"If you mean did I see silver threads, the universe in full technicolor, and an explosion that has me harder than a…," he cursed softly and nodded his head. "Yeah, I saw it. But—what does it mean?"

Marina slid her hand around to touched his cheek. "It means you are mine," she whispered.

Mike softly moaned in his sleep. The feeling of warmth against his cheek pulled at his consciousness. He had been locked in a dream that made him throb with more than a typical early morning hard-on. Marina's softly murmured words from last night rang through his mind along with the feel of her lips against his.

You are mine… You are mine… You are mine…

"Marina."

Her name slipped from his lips, and his head automatically turned to the warm breath that skimmed across his skin. He opened his mouth to murmur Marina's name again when a wet tongue, followed by the sounds of childish giggles, jerked him awake.

The moans quickly turned to a smothered curse as he pushed Charlie's furry face and eager tongue away. Sitting up, he ran the back of his hand across his mouth and glared at the excited pup that was now sitting in front of him with his tail going back and forth like a pendulum on steroids.

"Damn it, Charlie. You better not have been licking your balls or ass before you stuck that damn thing in my mouth," Mike growled.

Of course, that was like waving a juicy bone in front of the pup. Charlie leaned forward and licked the hand Mike had raised to protect his mouth. He turned his head when a soft, feminine laugh joined those of the group of children kneeling around him. Flushing, he dropped his hand to his lap when he saw Marina standing behind his curious audience. He raised his other hand instinctively to block Charlie when the pup tried to get his attention again.

"Morning," he said in a gruff voice.

"Good morning," Marina replied. She turned to her brother with a mischievous glint in her eye. "Geoff, would you mind taking the golden beast and the first group of children to the river to wash? Don't forget to set up guards this time," she instructed.

Geoff nodded and rose to his feet. "Yes. Come on, Charlie. You can help us protect the younger children."

Mike watched in silence as the group slowly made their way through the camp with Geoff and Charlie in the lead. He turned and rolled to his feet. He felt like he had just laid down on the thin pallet on the ground. It was late by the time he finally fell asleep. Part of his lack of sleep came from being overtired, but the majority of it came from what happened between him and Marina last night.

He bit back a groan as his muscles protested sleeping on the hard ground. *This is why air mattresses were invented,* he thought with a wry grin as he slowly stretched his stiff muscles. He was definitely getting too old for camping.

"I think Charlie has adopted your brother," he commented.

"Yes, I think you are right," she said, glancing everywhere but at him.

He watched as she shyly pushed back a strand of hair that had blown against her cheek. He couldn't stand the look of uncertainty in her eyes.

They had stayed up talking until after two in the morning. It wasn't until he realized Marina was struggling to keep her eyes open that he insisted they return to the camp and get some rest. Still, he hadn't resisted the urge to kiss her once more, just before she disappeared into the shelter where Erin lay sleeping. It hadn't been easy, but he had forced himself to turn and make his way to the pallet Geoff had set out for him.

When he got there, he had to push Charlie off his bed as usual. The Golden had been snoring almost as loudly as Geoff. After several minutes of pushing, Charlie had finally risen and moved over to lie next to the boy. In seconds, both of them were curled around each other, snoring away.

Mike had found himself staring up at the stars, trying to decipher the whirlwind of information that Marina had told him about her world and the Sea Witch. Another hour had passed before his brain finally rebelled. Exhausted, he fell into a restless slumber.

Pushing his thoughts away, he instinctively reached for Marina, pulling her into his arms. She stiffened at first before relaxing against him and burying her face against his shirt. Holding her close, he pressed a kiss to the top of her head.

"I thought a lot about what you told me last night. I want you to know that I'll do whatever I can to help you," he said, resting his cheek against her hair.

She pulled back and looked up at him with wide, hopeful eyes. "You'll see if the women are from your world and beg them to seek the help from the Dragon and the Sea King?" she whispered, gripping the sides of his shirt tightly in her fists.

Mike nodded. "Hell, if nothing else, I can at least close the two cases I was working on. I would rather find out they were married to some magical fairy tale creatures than find their bones scattered in the woods back in Oregon." he responded.

"Mike..." Marina started to say before she jerked in horror when she heard the loud screams coming from the nearby river. "The children!"

~

Marina's heart thundered in her chest and she gripped Mr. Bow tighter as she ran down the uneven path. Fear and self-reproach threatened to suffocate her. She swept her hand out, shattering the low, dead branch into that hung down dust. Behind her, she could hear Mike's steady breaths as he followed her.

She started to cry out in rage and frustration when Mike suddenly wrapped his hand around her arm and pulled her to a stop. Turning on him, her protest died on her lips when he shook his head in warning and held a finger to his lips. She realized he was right; charging into whatever lay ahead would just get them either caught or killed. She swallowed her protest and nodded, watching as he pulled his shiny silver and black weapon from its sheath.

She shivered when he stepped in front of her, his hands firmly clasped around the shiny weapon. He moved with a deadly purpose that spoke of an accomplished warrior. Charlie's frantic barking echoed through the air, mixing with the cries of some of the children.

They quietly moved up along a line of boulders that overlooked the river. Mike paused at the top, surveying the situation below. Marina knelt on the rough stone next to him. She frantically searched for her brother. Driven by fear when she didn't see him, she rose without thinking and lifted her bow as a low cry of fury escaped her.

Firing as fast as she could, she sent arrow after arrow into the beasts surrounding the children. Beside her, Mike rose up and fired his weapon at a Hellhound that had knocked Charlie onto his side and had the pup pinned to the ground. The creature rolled to the side before lying still in the shallow water of the river. Marina didn't hesitate, she fired three flaming arrows into the creature to make sure it was dead. The body glowed briefly before it turned to ash.

Sliding down the rock, she landed lightly on the rocky ground. Quickly scanning the area, she searched the dark shadows for more creatures. Mike landed beside her, turning so they were back to back as they made their way to the small group of children huddled together.

Marina turned her head to stare at the closest child. "Where's Geoff?" she demanded.

"They took him," one of the children replied in a shaking voice. "There were three of them. They came from the other side of the river and took us by surprise. Geoff told us to run when he saw them, but one of the Hellhounds blocked our path. He killed one before one of the Sea Witch's men knocked him unconscious and took him away. The… The ogre that took Geoff ordered the Hellhound to kill us."

"No," Marina's soft cry echoed as she sank to her knees.

Grief poured through her. Marina knew what the Sea Witch would do to her brother—turn him to stone if he didn't give her the information about the whereabouts of any others that opposed her. Marina bowed her head, closed her eyes, and breathed in and out deeply.

"Marina," Mike's husky voice pierced through the grief and rage threatening to overwhelm her.

Marina slowly opened her eyes, blinked back the burning tears, and looked up at Mike as he knelt on one knee in front of her. Her eyes began to burn again when she saw the worry and compassion in his eyes. Swallowing, she nodded and turned her face into his warm palm when he laid it against her cheek.

"I have to go after him," she whispered.

"*We* will go after him," Mike replied in a hard voice. "Together."

Marina slowly nodded and laid her hand into Mike's outstretched palm. They both rose to their feet. She moved her gaze to the children who were now petting Charlie. The pup's ears were drooping and there were traces of blood on his neck where the Hellhound had pinned him. He softly whined when he saw them staring at him.

"Take Charlie back to the camp and care for his wounds," Marina instructed in a low voice. "Tell Erin what happened and that we are going after Geoff."

"What about the others who have gone for food and wood?" a young girl asked in a trembling voice.

"Erin and Chia will know what to do," Marina assured the girl in a calm, steady voice that belied what she was really feeling.

The children nodded and turned away. Marina waited until they were out of sight before she turned to look at Mike. The expression on his face strengthened her belief that everything would work out. Whatever force of nature had brought him to her world, whether by a misspoken spell or fate intervening, she was glad he was by her side. She waited as he quickly ejected something from the weapon in his hand and checked it before sliding it back in.

"They will take him back to the palace. There are too many of them for us to fight," Marina said with a feeling of certainty.

"You said that this Drago and the Sea King might help," Mike said. "If nothing else, the Sea King is partly responsible for this mess. Can you contact him?"

She gave a stiff shake to her head. "I am young and still learning the magic of our people. This would require a power that I do not possess, but I know someone who can help us," she replied.

"Can you trust this person?" Mike asked in a steely voice.

"Yes. It will take a couple of hours to reach our destination," she said.

~

Mike watched as Marina turned on her heel and carefully crossed the stone path that created a natural bridge across the shallow river. Touching the gun pressed against his side, he made sure that it was secure as he followed her. He had three bullets left in the clip. While he did train to be a soldier in the Air Force, his field of expertise was internal investigations, not combat. Still, he continued his training and physical fitness once he left the military and joined the police force. He easily passed the physical requirements for the Police Department and was well trained for most situations. *Of course, they sure as hell didn't have training during his time in the military for dealing with magical creatures and things straight out of a horror movie,* he thought with a disgruntled sigh as he drew in a deep breath. *Hell, what I need is some Men in Black training, not that they ever had to deal with magic, just insane aliens. Still,* a part of his mind argued as he gazed at the woman ahead of him, *if I have to fight, I couldn't think of anyone better to be by my side than Marina. Though, I wouldn't mind having a couple of the guys from the force here as well.*

CHAPTER TWELVE

Mike watched as Marina wiped her hand over her cheek. Sweat glistened on her brow, but he knew the dampness she brushed away came from the stray tears that still escaped. Instinctively, he reached for her trembling fingers and squeezed them in encouragement.

"We'll get him back," Mike promised her in a low voice. "How much farther?"

"Not far," she replied, giving him a thankful smile before she focused on walking the path.

Mike nodded and released her fingers. He looked at the thick forest on each side of the path. They had covered a lot of ground over the past two hours, moving steadily down the high mountain to the valley far below. He had been surprised when Marina veered off the main road and onto a narrow path that looked more like an animal trail. They hadn't talked during their trip, instead conserving their energy to move deftly and silently along the difficult path. They had stopped twice to wait for some of the Sea Witch's ogres riding Hellhounds, to pass by. Each time, Marina had whispered a spell to conceal their presence. She said it was one of the spells her father had taught her when he realized what the Sea Witch was doing.

"Here," she murmured, stopping and looking to her left.

Mike frowned as he gazed in the same direction that Marina was looking. All he saw were thick trees and tall ferns. He was about to ask her if she was sure when she waved her right hand, as if pulling back a curtain. He knew his mouth was hanging open when the trees groaned and began to part.

"Holy...," Mike's voice died when he saw a manicured, pebble-covered path lined with a brilliant display of flowers. At the end of the path was a quaint little cottage straight out of a Thomas Kinkade painting. If the 'walking' trees weren't enough to stun him, the cry of the plants as they greeted Marina made him feel like he had fallen down the White Rabbit's hole, been swept up in a tornado, and deposited in the middle of an animated classic. "What next? The Giant from the beanstalk, along with his magic harp, and the goose that lays the golden eggs?" he muttered with a shake of his head.

"The Giants live on another Isle," Marina remarked, glancing over her shoulder. "Come, Grandmother is waiting for us."

"Your grandmother," Mike repeated, startled as he quickly stepped onto the path. He stumbled as he glanced over his shoulder. The trees were once again moving, this time closing the gap they had created. "Are you serious about the Giants?"

Marina frowned and nodded. "Of course," she replied. "I've never seen them in person, but Father and Mother have. They both said the giants are very nice, but rather rough around the edges."

"Marina! Come, child. Come inside," an elderly voice called out from the shadow of the doorway.

Mike stood frozen for a moment as he tried to wrap his head around Marina's casual acceptance of giants. Maybe they weren't the same as the fictional giants from back home. *Maybe they were just really, really, really tall people,* he thought with a grimace. With his luck, they were probably as real as this Drago the dragon and the Sea King merman!

"I am really going to need a drink by the time this adventure is over," he muttered under his breath before following Marina into the shelter.

Marina blushed when her grandmother looked at her with clouded eyes. She hadn't missed the inquisitive look or knowing smile when her grandmother tilted her head in Mike's direction. For the millionth time, Marina wondered how her grandmother seemed to see everything even though she knew the other woman was blind.

In the past year, she had only been able to come here twice to make sure her grandmother was safe. Marina sighed in regret as she gazed around the beautiful, quaint garden and tiny cottage. While she would have loved to create something like this for the children, she did not have the magical power to hide it the way her grandmother did. There had also been no way to bring all the children here to hide. To create an area big enough for everyone would have been too much for the enchanted garden and the ability of her grandmother's magic to conceal.

"Grandmother, this is Mike Hallbrook. He…." Marina started to say before stopping when her grandmother stepped up to Mike and gave him a kiss on both cheeks. Mike grinned and raised an eyebrow when her grandmother squeezed his arms.

"I know, I know. He is a stranger to our world. He's a strong one, child, and cute too! You are a very lucky witch. Now, both of you come in. I was just about to have a bite to eat," Ladonna Fae chuckled.

"Mike, may I present my grandmother, Ladonna. I have to caution you that she can be a bit blunt," Marina added under her breath when Mike stepped up to enter the cottage behind her grandmother.

"Nonsense. I am very blunt. At my age, I don't have to be socially polite anymore," Ladonna retorted, leaning on her cane.

"Hello, Ms. Cane," Mr. Bow greeted.

"Oh, no… You brought him back," Ms. Cane groaned.

Marina grimaced. She propped Mr. Bow up against the wall near the door. Turning, she saw Mike's questioning expression.

"Same forest, different trees. Another gift from my father," she quickly explained.

She closed the door and walked over to her grandmother who was placing a large pot of stew in the center of the table. There were three place settings already on the table. Her grandmother had known they were coming.

Marina retrieved the pitcher of water from the polished stone counter and placed it on the table. She looked up in surprise when Mike pulled out her chair. Murmuring her thanks, she slid onto the dark wooden seat. Her gaze followed him when he did the same for her grandmother.

Her grandmother's pleased hum told Marina that her grandmother was impressed with Mike's manners. He pulled out the chair to the right of her and sat down.

"We can talk about why you are here while we fill our bellies," Ladonna said with a wave of her hand.

The bowls in front of them floated over to the pot of stew. Ladonna continued to chat about the new flowers coming up in her garden while the ladle filled their bowls with the delicious smelling stew. Marina sliced thick sections of bread as the filled bowls landed in front of each person.

"I really should have planted the flowers on that side of the yard sooner. I don't know why I didn't think of it earlier," Ladonna sighed.

Marina waited until her grandmother finished speaking. She looked down at her bowl, suddenly not hungry. The thought of Geoff being in the Sea Witch's hands made her sick to her stomach. Closing her eyes, she tried to push the image of Isha and the others frozen in the courtyard out of her mind.

She opened her eyes and lifted her gaze up to Mike. He squeezed her fingers under the table in support. She gave him a grateful smile before turning her attention back to her grandmother who had grown silent.

"Grandmother, one of the Sea Witch's ogres took Geoff," she quietly informed the older woman.

"Yes, I know, child," Ladonna replied. "That is why you are here."

"Yes."

Marina blinked back the tears in her eyes. Her grandmother reached over and patted Marina's hand. The older woman sighed and nodded to them to eat.

"Food first. You will need your strength on the journey you have ahead of you," Ladonna instructed.

"I came to ask for your help. I created a portal between our world and Mike's. I… I don't know how I did it, but if there is a way to do it again—this time to the Isle of the Sea Serpent—we hoped to ask for the Sea King's help," Marina explained.

"Portals can be tricky. Lucky for you, I know a thing or two about them. Now, do not worry so, child. Everything will work out," her grandmother said as she blew on the hot mixture.

"How can you be so sure?" Marina asked.

Ladonna turned her head toward Mike. "Your young man has powerful magic, but it will take the combined strength of the Sea King, the King of the Dragons, and Magna herself to defeat the evil that controls our kingdom," she explained.

"What are you talking about? Why would Magna help defeat herself?" Marina asked in confusion.

"The Sea Witch either made one vital error when she cast her spell or she did it on purpose," Ladonna said.

Marina frowned. "I know that she retreats to the palace each night because of the spell that drains us. I suspected that was why she disappeared each day before the sun sets," Marina said with an impatient wave of her hand. "What use is that if we are too tired and weak to do anything? Even the Sea King and Drago will more than likely suffer from the effects!"

"Yes, Magna's spell affects her just as much as it does the rest of us, except for your young man. Magna is just as much a product of the magic of our Isle as she is of the sea. She needs both to survive, but the creature that has possessed her can only survive inside her or inside someone else."

Marina frowned and laid her spoon down. "What creature? What are you talking about?" she demanded.

"I see, though I am blind, Marina, many things that others do not. Isha came to visit me before he was turned to stone. My visions are oft times not as clear as I would wish. I told him the same thing that I tell you now. The Sea Witch is not all that she appears. There is something darker living inside her—something alien to our world. I still see the young girl she used to be locked inside. Magna fights the evil imprisoning her as best she can. Have you never wondered why Magna would create a spell that happens to weaken her as well as others? One that would force her, the Hellhounds, and the ogres back to the palace when darkness falls?" Ladonna asked.

"I—I thought it was just to protect her when she was at her weakest. I was just so grateful that it gave us some measure of relief from the constant threat of attack," Marina admitted.

Ladonna shook her head. "The spell she cast upon the ogres fades, and she must lock them up so they cannot escape. The Hellhounds are unnatural beasts. They are made from the darker magic feeding on hers. They guard her at night when she is defenseless," she explained.

"Do you mind if I ask how you can be sure of this information?" Mike interjected when he saw Marina mulling over these details.

"Because I have one of the ogres. They are quite talkative beasts when you get to know them. I found him stuck in the tar pit and took pity on him once darkness fell and he turned back to his normal self," Ladonna explained with a wry grin on her face. "I've always had a soft spot for the creatures. No one can grow mushrooms like they can."

"Grandmother, you could have been captured or worse! Where is he now?" Marina asked in horror, leaning forward and placing her hand on her grandmother's arm. "During the day he could still harm you."

Ladonna shook her head, her clouded eyes swirling with color. "Magna is not the only powerful witch on this Isle," she said with a shake of her head. "While I'm not as strong as I used to be, I can still protect my home and gardens."

Marina sat back in her chair. "That is why we need your help. Only the King and Queen together would have been strong enough to defeat Magna. If she had not tricked the King and imprisoned the Queen with her deceit, none of this would have happened."

"No, child, not even they could have stopped her. It will take more than magic to defeat her. You will be able to see the evil that is inside her. You must not let it escape. If it does, it will only move to another. There is one who is more powerful than even Magna. You must make sure that the evil inside Magna does not touch the Keeper of Lost Souls," Ladonna whispered, staring straight ahead, as if she could see into the future.

"Lost souls?" Mike asked, leaning forward and resting his elbows on the table. "Marina mentioned the Sea King and Drago. Can they defeat Magna?"

"Defeat, no, but they can free her and the rest of the Seven Kingdoms with help from you and Marina," Ladonna said.

"Then, we have to talk to them," Marina insisted.

She pushed away from her half-eaten meal and rose to her feet. Her hands clenched in determination. She would do whatever it took to free her family and her people.

Ladonna sighed and nodded. With a wave of her wrinkled hand, the dishes on the table disappeared and a set of brilliant green and blue stones appeared. Ladonna slowly rose, the chair behind her quickly stepping backwards out of her way, and nodded for Marina to pick up the stones.

"I store some of my magic in the stones. Remember, you must convince the Sea King and Drago to attack before the dawn of a new day. Once Magna's spell lifts, she will be too powerful and will have the armies of the ogres and Hellhounds to protect her. Be careful, though. If the creature inside her feels threatened, it may destroy the stone statues held prisoner. If that happens, the King and Queen will be lost forever. Take the stones and place them in a circle and repeat after me," Ladonna instructed.

Marina nodded. She scooped the stones up into her hands. Carrying them, she quickly moved to stand in front of the hearth. Handing some of the stones to Mike, they carefully laid them on the worn rug in a circle and stepped inside. Marina held one hand out to Mike. He placed his hand on hers, and she grasped it firmly. Turning, she called to Mr. Bow to come to her. Once she had a grip on both Mike and her bow, she murmured to her grandmother that they were ready.

"Be safe, child, and remember, I will always be in your heart," Ladonna whispered before she began chanting in a low voice.

Marina's gaze jerked to her grandmother's face. She parted her lips in protest, but no words would come. The serene look on her grandmother's face etched into her memory as her grandmother began to weave her spell. Through the swirling colors of magic, she could see her grandmother begin to fade.

She trembled as the quaint cottage shimmered, growing old and crumbling before her eyes. The outside gardens became visible. Near the creek, the ogre that her grandmother had saved looked up from where he was tending a small bed of mushrooms. Deep sorrow darkened his eyes as his features began to change. The protection of her grandmother's magic faded, and he was once again bewitched with the Sea Witch's curse. Her grandmother gave the last of her magic to Marina.

"I love you, child. Save our kingdom and tell your father that I will miss him, but will always be there in his heart," Ladonna whispered.

"Grandmother…."

Marina's soft cry of protest faded with the last of the magical garden that her grandmother had created. She closed her eyes and focused on the magic swirling around Mike and herself. She felt his hand tighten on hers as the colors of the magic began to change to those of rich wood and stone.

A hoarse sob caught in her throat, and she forced herself to stand strong as the wave of grief swept through her. Silent tears coursed down her cheeks, and she had to blink to clear her vision. Her gaze swept around the room before returning to Mike when he swayed and bent forward to brace his hands on his knees. Resting her hand on his back, her gaze locked with a pair of brilliant light blue eyes.

"The Sea King," she whispered.

CHAPTER THIRTEEN

Mike swallowed down the wave of nausea that churned in his stomach. That damn portal should come with a warning label that said 'Intense, swirling colors may cause nausea and disorientation'. He took a deep breath when he felt Marina's hand on his back.

"I'm okay," he muttered, taking another deep breath and slowly straightening.

"The Sea King," Marina murmured.

"Oh shit," Mike said, freezing when he saw that they weren't alone. Not only were they not alone, they were surrounded by a large group of people. He rolled his shoulders, wincing when he felt his stomach twist in protest for a moment. "Marina…"

"I know," she responded in a soft voice. She wiped the dampness from her cheeks and turned until she was facing the tall figure standing on the platform above them. "Your Majesty, I beg forgiveness for intruding on you without warning, but my people need your help."

"Detective Hallbrook?!" a startled feminine voice said.

"Shit, she *is* here!" Mike whispered, staring at the redhead standing next to the man on the platform. "Jenny Ackerly."

"Who are you?" the male demanded as he stepped in front of Jenny.

"Your Majesty, please… I beg a moment of your time. I am Marina Fae, a witch from the Isle of Magic. Our visit here came at a… at a great cost. Please, we need your help," Marina said.

Mike saw a tear slowly slip down Marina's cheek. He wrapped his arm around her and pulled her close to him. His sharp gaze met that of the man watching them.

"My name is Mike Hallbrook. We must speak with you about an urgent matter," he added, shifting everyone's attention to him when he sensed that Marina needed a moment to contain her grief.

Personally, Mike didn't give a damn who the man was as long as he could help them. He could feel Marina tremble under his touch. Something had happened as they were leaving. He'd heard Marina's strangled cry and saw everything changing around them as the colors intensified.

"Kapian, clear the room," the Sea King ordered.

Mike watched as another man stepped forward. He heard the doors open behind him and the excited voices of people as they filed out of the room. He turned his gaze to the woman slowly descending the steps. It was obvious from the smothered curse of the king that he wasn't happy about her decision.

"Jenny," the Sea King growled in exasperation.

"It's okay, Orion. Detective Hallbrook is not a threat," Jenny said.

Mike waited until she stopped in front of him. He released Marina and reached for Jenny's extended hand. She held it for a moment, studying his expression.

"You really are here," she breathed.

"Yes. We need the Sea King's help and that of a man named Drago. It is important," Mike replied.

"Orion, I think we should have this discussion somewhere more comfortable," Jenny said, releasing Mike's hand and looking with concern at Marina's distraught face.

Orion's lips twisted in disapproval. "You are from my wife's world," he stated more than asked.

"Yes," Mike replied, gripping the other man's hand in a tight handshake.

"How did you get here?" he demanded.

"It is a long story but a very interesting one," Mike replied.

Orion gazed intently at Mike, trying to read him, and must have been satisfied with what he saw. The other man gave a brief nod and released his hand.

"I look forward to hearing it. But know this—Jenny stays here. If you try to take her back with you, I will kill you," Orion warned.

Mike raised an eyebrow at the threat. "My job is to find her and make sure she is safe. It is up to her if she wishes to stay," he replied with a shrug.

Orion nodded. "Follow me."

Mike wrapped his arm around Marina's waist again. She leaned against him and sniffed. They waited until Orion and Jenny were several steps ahead before following them. The man Orion called Kapian followed at a slight distance behind them.

"What happened?" Mike quietly asked.

Marina drew in a deep breath before releasing it in a shuddering sigh. She wiped at the fresh tears that escaped. Concerned, he wished they could stop for a moment so he could hold her.

"Grandmother… gave us the last of her magic. She… she has passed on to the next life," she said in a halting voice.

Regret flashed through him. Uncaring of what Orion or the others thought, he stopped and pulled Marina into his arms, holding her tightly against him. Pressing his lips to the top of her head, he gently rubbed her back.

"I have lost so many of my family. When will this ever stop?" she choked out.

"Soon. We'll convince this Sea King and Drago to help us. We'll free your brothers and parents. I won't stop until they are free," Mike promised.

He lifted his gaze and he stared intently at Orion. The other man had turned to see why they stopped. The grim expression on Orion's face and the one of compassion on Jenny's told him that they had overheard Marina's impassioned, choked plea.

Marina trembled before she took a deep breath and composed herself. Mike tenderly wiped the dampness from her cheeks with his thumbs and leaned forward to brush a light, gentle kiss across her lips. She gave him a wavering smile of thanks. Turning to look at Orion and Jenny, she briefly bowed her head.

"My apologies, your Majesties," she said.

"No apologies are necessary. It is I who should apologize." Orion looked at the man standing quietly behind them. "Kapian, send a message to Drago. Tell him the time has come. He will understand. This time, we will not stop until my cousin is vanquished."

"Right away, your Majesty. I will also assemble an elite team of warriors," Kapian stated before he turned on his heel and strode off.

Mike watched the man named Kapian disappear down the long corridor. He turned back to Orion and Jenny. Jenny had walked over to grasp Marina's hand.

"I can't wait to hear how you met Detective Hallbrook and how he ended up here," Jenny said with a smile.

"Call me Mike. I have to admit I'm a little curious as well. Do you know if Carly Tate is here?" Mike asked.

Jenny nodded. "Oh yes. She is married to Drago," she said with a huge grin.

"Let us retire to a more comfortable area to discuss what has happened," Orion suggested, wrapping his arm around Jenny's waist.

"Thank you," Mike replied.

~

"I guess you've been searching for me in addition to Carly since I disappeared," Jenny said as she handed a drink to Mike.

"Yeah. I have to admit this has been one of the strangest events of my life," Mike said.

"Tell me about it! If anyone had ever told me that I would end up in a magical world and fall for a merman, I'd have pointed them to the nearest door or maybe a psych ward," Jenny replied, sitting down in the chair across from him.

His eyes strayed to where Marina and Orion were quietly talking. He could hear their conversation and understood that the Sea King wanted to hear what had happened over the past year. His stomach clenched as Marina shared the horrors of trying to keep herself and the group of children safe.

"So, is he really the Sea King? I mean, is it just a name or is he really a… you know…." Mike waved his hand as if he was swimming.

"Yes, he really is a merman," Jenny replied, looking over at Orion with an expression that showed her love for the man. "So am I, now."

Mike turned back to look at Jenny with a startled look. "He turned you into a mermaid?" he asked in surprise.

"Well, my legs don't change into a tail; but yes, I can swim and breathe under the water like a mermaid just as Carly can change into a dragon and fly," Jenny said with a grin, her eyes sparkling with amusement. "Yesterday, one of her kids came down with a cold, and Drago insisted that they return home, or you would have met them today."

Mike took a deep swallow of his drink before he lowered the glass to the table. Mermaids, dragons, witches, Hellhounds, ogres, and the list just kept growing. He studied Jenny's glowing features as she bent over to pick up the infant lying in the bassinet who had begun to fuss.

He didn't need to ask if she was happy here. The contented smile on her lips was more than enough of an answer. From the little she had mentioned of Carly, it would appear the other missing woman was just as happy.

He moved his gaze to where Marina was standing near the balcony doors. A warm glow spread through his body. He now realized the attraction he was feeling for Marina was deeper than infatuation. He was falling in love with her.

"Do you think Orion will help us?" he asked in a quiet voice.

Jenny nodded, glancing at Orion as he listened to Marina with a tight expression. "Yes," she replied in a confident tone. "Yes. He knows Magna is his responsibility. He told me that she changed years ago when they were teenagers. He doesn't understand why, but he realizes that it is his responsibility to stop her."

"I wasn't going to ask, but well… This world is so different from ours. How do you know for sure you would be happy here?" Mike asked.

His gaze remained on Marina. Her expression relaxed, and she nodded as she listened to Orion. He could see the relief in her eyes and some of the tension fade from her body.

"Do we ever really know until we try?" she asked with a raised eyebrow. "Yes, this world is different, but falling in love and having a family is the same—as long as you can get over the fact that your new in-laws may be mermaids, dragons, witches, or even monsters, that is.

I couldn't imagine ever returning to our world—especially now," Jenny replied, looking down at her daughter. "I belong here. What about you? I see the way you look at Marina and the way she looks at you. Life is very different for people here. Someone like Orion could never survive in our world. It would be too dangerous."

"I honestly never even thought of Marina coming to our world. Hell, I still don't understand how I got here," Mike admitted.

"Magna was instrumental in my being here. The day after I talked to you, I returned to Yachats State Park to search for clues regarding Carly's disappearance. I didn't find anything, of course. I had made up my mind that it was time to let go." She shook her head and turned to look over at Orion. "I've always loved the water. I walked down to the beach and, a short time later, I heard Dolph, Orion's oldest son, laughing." She turned to look back at Mike, a soft smile curved her lips. "He later said he had just about given up on finding a fiery-haired woman to be his mother when he spotted me walking along the beach. When he ran into the water, I followed. I was afraid he would drown. The next thing I knew, I was in this world," she finished.

"Do you know if there is a way back?" Mike asked.

Jenny shrugged. "I suppose if there is a way here, there is a way back. Carly told me that she was hiking along the trail when she got caught in a thunderstorm. There was a crack in the side of the mountain that opened into what looked like a small cave. She squeezed through it. The next thing she knew, she had stumbled onto Drago's hoard of treasure." Jenny chuckled and shook her head. "Carly is the only person I know who could end up in a cave filled with gold and only see the dragon. She told me that Drago told her to pick her treasure wisely and didn't know what to think when she asked if she could keep him."

"Do you think the Sea Witch had anything to do with Carly being here?" Mike asked.

"I don't know. I honestly don't know what to think of the woman. It is like she has two different personalities. One part of her is good, she helped Juno at one point, while another part of her is pure evil," she said.

"I will help Marina and her people. If Drago is going to help, he will be here by dawn," Orion said.

"Remember what Nali said," Jenny warned.

Orion nodded. "I remember. That is why I am sending requests to the other rulers as well," he said.

"Other rulers?" Mike asked, confused.

Marina came over and sat down in the chair next to Mike. She still gripped Mr. Bow tightly in her hands. Mike leaned over and took one of her hands in his.

"The Sea King is going to ask for help from the King of the Giants, the Empress of the Monsters, the Pirate King, and the Elementals," Marina explained.

"The Empress of the Monsters.... I can't wait to see who else shows up," Mike repeated with a shake of his head.

CHAPTER FOURTEEN

"I hope you will be comfortable. If you need anything, you have only to ask," the young woman named Karin said with a smile.

Marina nodded. She swallowed when the woman closed the door, suddenly feeling lost and very much alone. Unsure of what to do, she turned around to look at the large, elegant bedroom that she was given. Marina had never been in such an ornately decorated room. A fireplace almost large enough to stand in was centered on one wall. In the hearth, a magical fire merrily crackled and popped, sending out a welcome warmth.

Across from the fireplace was a huge four-poster bed. Each post was elaborately carved to look like coral. Marina noticed a long nightgown and robe across the foot of the bed and a pair of silk slippers on the floor beneath.

There was a set of double doors, standing open, and leading out onto the balcony. On each side of the doors, a column of windows rose from floor to ceiling, giving the occupant a magnificent view of the twinkling lights from the city below. A short distance from the city the ocean waves crashed against the cliffs, the sound was soothing. There was another door on the opposite side of the room that Marina suspected led into the bathing room.

With a loud sigh, she walked over to the fireplace and gazed down at the dancing flames. She hugged Mr. Bow tightly against her chest and bit her lip in uncertainty.

"You know, if you keep holding me this tightly, I might think you are dreaming that I'm Mike," Mr. Bow dryly stated.

"What? Oh, I'm sorry, Mr. Bow," Marina murmured, loosening her grip.

"Why don't you go to him?" Mr. Bow asked.

Marina shook her head. "And do what? Tell him that I want to feel his lips upon mine? That I want to feel his arms wrapped around me, and…."

She blushed and placed Mr. Bow on the table near the fireplace. She closed her eyes as a wave of desire swept through her with such intensity that it caused a physical ache. Perhaps she should tell him that she desired him in a way that she had never felt before. She knew that Mike wanted her. The evidence of his attraction to her had been obvious when he'd kissed her and she'd felt his hips pressed against hers.

"And… what?"

Marina's eyes flew open, and she gasped and quickly turned at the sound of Mike's deep voice. Her gaze locked with his. He stood in the open doorway leading out onto the balcony.

"I…," Marina's voice faded when she saw the burning desire in his eyes.

"And what, Marina?" he asked again.

The rough need in his voice washed over her. Once again the piercing desire swept through her, causing the ache to grow to a pulsing heat between her legs. He was her match—the other part of herself—he completed her.

"You can see my magic. You can feel it," she said, hoping he would understand what she was saying.

"I see the colors that surround you wrapping around me." He lifted his hand up and took a step toward her. He turned his hand, staring at it. Marina could see the colors of her magic, uninhibited by Magna's spell, swirling around him. "I can feel the connection to you," he murmured, turning his gaze back to her.

"I need you, Mike. I want you in a way I've never wanted to be with another," she confessed, taking a step toward him.

~

They moved slowly toward each other. As the gap between them narrowed, Marina's magic spun outward, cloaking them in the warmth of her aura. Mike sucked in a deep breath as he felt the unusual power flow through him. This was different from a runner's high, this was like seeing the universe opened up before you and being able to walk among the stars.

A soft hiss escaped him when Marina finally touched him. Her hands moved up his chest to cup his cheeks. He could see the uncertainty and a trace of vulnerability in her eyes. With a soft moan, he lowered his head and captured her lips.

The spark that had ignited before between them burst into a raging wildfire. Mike could feel Marina's hands sliding along his skin to his hair. Her fingers splayed, holding him to her while her lips and tongue explored his mouth.

A soft moan escaped him when her hands moved down along his neck and over his shoulders. He tried to pull back, but every time he did, she would follow him. Her hands were driving him crazy. They ran up and down his arms before moving around to his back.

She didn't stop there. He sucked in a deep breath when she pulled both of his shirts free and slid her hands up under them to his heated flesh. Reaching around, he gripped her wrists and pulled back while his eyes shone with the fire burning inside him.

"I need a shower or a bath or whatever in the hell you take here," he muttered in frustration.

Marina's eyes glittered. Her fingers curled around his, and she tugged him toward a door on the opposite side of the room. Mike knew he was in trouble when she opened the door to the bathroom. His resolve to be a gentleman was quickly melting away. If she did what he was hoping for, there would be no stopping or going back.

"Marina," he tried to warn her.

She looked at him with a fierce expression. "You say you need to bathe. I wish to bathe with you," she said, pausing in the doorway.

"Honey, if we go in there, I can assure you there is going to be a lot more than bathing going on," Mike warned.

"I hope there will be," Marina softly admitted, starting to turn back to step inside.

Mike pulled her to a stop. She turned, a faint expression of doubt creeping into her eyes. He reached up and cupped her cheek.

"This isn't going to be a one night stand—or even a two night stand. If I make love to you, Marina, it will be for keeps," he said.

"I… I have never asked to be with a man before, Mike Hallbrook," Marina admitted, flushing and glancing over his shoulder.

Mike bit back the curse that almost slipped out. He had suspected that Marina was inexperienced, but he hadn't realized that she might be a virgin. Swallowing, he dropped his hand to his side and clenched his fist. This was going to be a true test of his willpower.

"We come from two different worlds," Mike said.

Marina's gaze jerked back to his face. "Does it bother you that we are different?" she asked.

He shook his head. "No, but I want you to be sure. I meant what I said, Marina—especially now. If I take you tonight, this is serious," he said, emphasizing the last word.

"When you take me tonight, we will be together as one," she retorted in a quiet voice.

"Damn woman, you are going to drive me over the edge," Mike cursed, wrapping his hand around her braid and capturing her lips again.

He didn't resist the tug this time when she pulled him into the bathroom. His mind played through all the ways he wanted to make love to her. Knowing that this was her first time, he was going to do everything he could to make sure she enjoyed it. That included making sure she knew that he liked to have a little fun. He had always been an intense—but selective—lover. Something told him that Marina, even inexperienced as she was, would have no trouble keeping up with him.

Breaking the kiss, he stepped back. His eyes glittered with promise, and his cock felt like he could drive nails with it. It had been a long time since he was this aroused. If he didn't take some control of the situation soon, it could quickly spiral into raw, primitive sex.

"Take off your clothes," he ordered.

"Only if you also remove yours," she countered, lifting her chin.

Mike raised an eyebrow at her daring tone. The curve of her lips proved that she might be innocent of the actual act, but she knew what was about to happen. His suspicion proved accurate when her eyes twinkled with mischief, and she started to unfasten her top.

"I may live in a small village, but I have visited the capital city many times. What I have not seen during my trips, my mother and grandmother made sure to add to my education when I was old enough and curious enough to ask. Grandmother was a little more enlightening than my mother," she explained with a wicked grin.

"How enlightening?" Mike asked, his gaze mesmerized by her fingers as she continued to undress.

"Very," she informed him with an inviting look.

Marina undid the last button and turned her back to him before she slowly shrugged her blouse off one shoulder. She paused to glance at him with a teasing smile before slipping it off the other shoulder. He swallowed when he saw that she didn't wear anything underneath her top. Her fingers moved to her belt, and she slowly tugged it free from her pants.

When she held it up in the air, Mike reached out and took the belt, wrapping it around his hand. She turned her head to stare at him again over her shoulder.

"Grandmother told me that to receive great passion and pleasure, you need to enjoy it the same way that you enjoy a good wine," she murmured.

Mike swallowed. Her fingers were moving down along her side to her leggings. He could see the curve of her creamy breast, but not the tantalizing nipple that made his mouth water when he thought of what the hard tip would feel like when he sucked on it.

"And how do you… enjoy a good wine?" he asked in a rough voice.

"By teasing your taste buds, having the right dish to go with it, and savoring it so that it lasts all night," she whispered.

Mike's soft rumble of approval echoed through the bathroom when Marina pulled off each boot as she spoke before pushing down her leggings. They slid down her long legs to pool at her ankles. She lifted one foot and pulled it free before kicking off the other leg.

"Kelia prepared my bath. Will you join me, Mike?" Marina asked.

Mike watched her walk over to the raised platform. She stepped into the bath, and turned, allowing him to see her for the first time.

She was slender from the challenges of the last year, but still completely feminine. Her breasts were small and firm. She had a short waist, but long legs that made his hips jerk at the thought of them wrapped around him. His gaze traveled down to the patch of dark brown curly hair between her legs.

His mouth watered at all the wonderful things he planned for that part of her body. He quickly pulled off his shirts, untied and pulled off his boots and socks, and shucked his pants. His wicked smile lit up his eyes when he heard her swiftly inhaled breath at the first sight of his throbbing cock.

"I think it is time that I began enjoying my wine," he teased, climbing up onto the platform.

"Ye… Yes, it is," she agreed, sinking back into the water.

"How hot do you like it, Marina?" Mike asked, stepping into the water.

"The… the water?" she mumbled, her eyes glued to his cock.

Mike chuckled, sank down into the water, and reached for her. "The sex," he murmured, pressing his lips against her neck.

A soft moan echoed in the room. "Hot… very, very hot," she said, unaware of anything but his lips against her heated flesh.

CHAPTER FIFTEEN

Marina suspected she knew what Mike meant about hot. If her suspicions were correct, she was ready. Her body felt like it was on fire. She never expected that teasing him the way she had would cause her body to react the way it did.

She tilted her head back and shivered despite the heated water swirling around them. She parted her legs to straddle Mike when he pulled her toward him. When she felt his cock brush across her womanhood, a shaft of intense desire pierced her, starting between her legs and moving through her entire body with a speed that left her gasping.

Instinctively, she gripped his shoulders and rose up on her knees to join them together. A groan of frustration escaped her when he reached out and wrapped his hands around her waist—effectively stopping her from impaling herself on him. On a positive note, the move aligned her breast with his mouth.

"You make my insides melt," she whimpered.

He turned his head and locked his lips around her straining nipple.

"Yes!" she cried.

The feel of his lips tugging on her pebbled tips felt so much better than when she used her fingers. Bowing her head, she watched him roll his tongue over the taut, rosy crest.

"The other… It is feeling neglected," she ordered hoarsely.

Mike's soft, warm breath caressed her cool flesh when he released her. "You are a bossy little thing. I like it," he growled before capturing her other nipple.

"Oh! It does things between my legs," she said, her nails curling against his shoulders.

"Let's see what other feelings I can make you have," he murmured against her breast.

"Other…," she choked out on a hiccup.

The other was his hand moving from her waist to the mound between her legs. His fingers teased her, running along the soft folds that protected her. When he brushed against her swollen nub, she quivered.

"I'm going to wash you, Marina. I want to take my time exploring you," Mike said against her damp skin.

"Can we… can we not wait to do the exploring later?" she breathed in an unsteady voice.

"Oh, no, my impatient little witch. The first time is all about torture by pleasure," he chuckled, turning her in his arms. "And I plan to torture you until you scream."

Marina gripped the side of the large tub and held on when he ran his hands down along her arms and pressed them to the rim of the tub. His hands slid back down and he gripped her hips, pulling her buttocks up and spreading her legs. Her fingers curled when he ran both hands over the cheeks of her ass.

"I've always been a breast and butt man," he informed her.

"I… That is nice… good… to know…," she replied. "What are you going to do?" she asked, licking her lips after she heard the water splash when he rose up.

"Will you trust me?" he asked.

Marina's eyes locked with his in the mirror on the far wall. She could see everything he was doing. There was something extremely erotic about watching what was happening while experiencing it. She followed him with her eyes as he picked up a bar of the lightly scented soap. The aroma of fresh Evergreens reached her when he dampened the bar and began rubbing it between his hands.

He replaced the bar and turned those mesmerizing hands on her next. Goosebumps rose over her skin before quickly fading when he began to run his soapy hands up under her from her lower hips along her stomach and up to her breasts where he teased them to full peaks again. A gasp escaped her when he tweaked them.

"Sometimes a little light pain can lead to a great deal of pleasure," he explained.

"How can pain…? Oh! That is how," she exclaimed when he tweaked them again before pinching her nipples and rolling his fingers.

Marina bit her lip to keep from crying out when Mike continued his sensual assault on her body. His hands ran along her arms, washing her all the way from shoulder to fingertips before he drew her back against his body to rinse her. She relaxed against him when he picked up the soap again. This time she was sitting on his lap. He had his feet hooked around her ankles, holding her legs apart. It was the feel of his cock pulsing against her ass that had her hips rocking, though.

Her head fell back against his shoulder when he began washing her chest and stomach. His fingers paused, taking time to make sure that her nipples remained hard and throbbing. She rose up when he pinched the taut tips hard between his fingers, and he rose with her, pressing his cock along the lining of her ass.

"Can you feel how much I want you?" he murmured, brushing a kiss along her shoulder as his hands moved down to her soft curls.

"I want you," she whimpered.

Want was an understatement, she decided. She craved him. Her body felt like it no longer belonged to her. Every inch was super-sensitive and places she didn't know could hurt, did—in a very pleasurable way.

She spread her legs when he began stroking her. He was rubbing against her nub while playing with her breast. The heat rushing through her had nothing to do with the warm water and everything to do with what Mike was doing to her.

"Mike... Mike... Ah!!!" her voice rose and her body stiffened.

She had felt this rush before but never with such an intensity. The books her grandmother had given her had always mentioned seeing the flashing of lights behind closed eyes and mind-numbing pleasure, but she had always thought the author had penned a gross exaggeration of the feelings one could feel.

As her body melted against his, she decided that she was the one who had been in error. The feelings were much more intense. She groaned when his fingers slipped from her still throbbing clit, and he turned her in his arms.

"This is just the beginning," he promised when she looked at him with a dazed expression.

"Does that mean it is my turn to wash you?" she purred, fingering his hair on the back of his head as she rubbed against his hard cock.

"Son of a...."

Marina captured Mike's soft expletive with her lips. If the stories she read were true, she could give as much pleasure to him as he had given to her. She planned to do a little exploring herself to find out.

~

Mike drew in a deep breath when Marina ran her hands up and down his chest. She curled her fingers in his dark, coarse hair and gently tugged on it. He lowered his eyelids when she moved them over his nipples. They were hard and extremely sensitive.

He hissed out the breath he was holding when she flicked them with her fingernail. His cock jerked under her rolling hips. The feel of her soft flesh rubbing along his long shaft made him grit his teeth.

She leaned forward and brushed her breasts back and forth against his chest. Her lips paused a breath away from his, and her eyes glittered with fierce desire. For a moment, Mike wondered if he had died back on the beach and somehow landed in this perfect afterlife.

"I want to wash you," she murmured against his lips. "And taste you."

"Damn!" Mike swore, closing his eyes when she reached down between them and wrapped her hand around his blood-engorged cock.

His head fell back as she stroked him. He could hear her picking up the bar of soap. Seconds later, she ran the bar across his chest and shoulders. While she washed him with one hand, she continued to glide from the tip of his ultra-sensitive head down to the base of his rock-hard sack with the other.

He lifted his arm when she ran her hand up under it before sliding down across his stomach. His hips moved up and down, not pausing when she briefly held him with a double fisted grip.

He groaned and opened his eyes when she pulled back, releasing his cock and sliding her hands along his parted thighs. She smiled at him with confidence built on the knowledge that she held him completely enthralled. Licking her bottom lip, she motioned for him to turn around and stand.

Mike did as she bade. He made sure that his cock brushed against her parted lips. That move turned out to be a huge mistake when her tongue darted out and she swiped the tip of it.

"Marina...," he warned, clenching his fists.

"Not yet," she replied with a secretive smile. "You deserve to feel the pleasure as well."

He growled under his breath and turned when she stood up and placed her hands on his hips. Mike looked down, following her hand as she picked up the bar of soap once again. He wished there was a mirror on the wall he was facing like there was on the other side. All he could do was close his eyes and imagine what she looked like standing behind him rubbing her hands over his shoulders and down his back to his buttocks. He stiffened when he felt her fingers trail along the crevice.

"I think I might be attracted to your ass as well," she said, pressing her breasts against his back and running her soapy hands down between his cheeks.

"Damn woman! I'm never going to make it if you keep this up," he muttered in a hoarse voice.

"We have all night," she murmured.

All night was not going to be enough for him. She slid her soapy hands around his waist and double-fisted his cock again. He bowed his head and opened his eyes, watching with pleasure as she slid her hands back and forth. The tip of his cock was so full that beads of pre-cum seeped from the bluish-purple, bulbous tip. A shudder ran through him when her fingers brushed over the tiny slit.

"I won't make it," he exclaimed in a harsh voice, reaching down and gripping her wrists. He turned in her arms, his face taut as he fought for control. "Rinse and bend over the side."

Marina sank down into the water. Mike followed her, rinsing the soap from his body. His hand gripped his cock. He squeezed his throbbing penis, hoping to hold off his need to come so that he could make her come again. That hope faded when she rose and pulled the towel laid out to the side close enough that she could lean her elbows on it. Her beautiful ass was raised in the air and he could see the swollen folds part.

Kneeling behind her, he spread her lips and pressed two fingers into her, stretching her while using his thumb to play with her damp clit. He bent forward and nipped her left cheek. As he'd hoped, slick moisture guided his fingers deeper. Stroking her, he pushed deeper and deeper until he felt the thin membrane barrier.

He slid his fingers free and rose up behind her. He guided his cock to her channel, the film of his pre-cum mixing with moisture. They were both more than ready. He slid the tip of his cock inside her, pausing to give her time to adjust.

His legs trembled as he watched his cock slowly disappear. He could feel her tight channel wrapping around him. Sliding his hands to her hips, he held her rocking hips still to give him time to regain control.

"I'll try not to hurt you," he said in a strained voice, locking his eyes with hers in the mirror.

"Pleasure can be painful sometimes," she whispered, staring back at him with unblinking eyes as she pushed back.

"Damn, Marina," Mike cried out, feeling his cock slip deeper inside her.

The thread of his control snapped when he felt the barrier separating them break, and he leaned forward, caging her beneath him. He released her hips to cup her breasts as he began to rock with a primitive need to mark and claim the woman as his.

He pinched her nipples, watching the flash of pain turn to immediate pleasure as he drove into her. He released one breast to slide his hand down between her legs. He found the sensitive spot he was searching for and began to stroke it to the same intense rhythm of his thrusts.

Her fingers splayed around the smooth tile surrounding the tub, and she thrust her hips back, encouraging him to take her without restraint. As she came, her long, loud cry echoed through the room. Her canal squeezed his cock with such pressure that he swore they were no longer two people but one.

He rocked his hips faster and faster despite her body's resistance in allowing him to pull out. The bulbous tip sank deep, and he felt the powerful force of his seed spilling from him. He ground his hips against her buttocks, pushing as deep as his cock could go. Behind his closed eyelids, he saw the white sparks connecting with strands of brilliant color. The threads arced outward, wrapping around their bodies.

Falling forward, he placed his hands along either side of Marina's body, holding her pinned beneath him. His body was still locked to hers. They were both breathing heavily, and he could feel her trembling.

"Will it always be like this?" she whispered, her head bowed and her eyes closed.

"Something tells me it will be even better," he murmured, pressing a kiss to her shoulder.

"I would like that," she answered with a sigh.

~

An hour later, Mike gently laid Marina in the large bed. She turned and snuggled up against him when he slid in beside her. He wrapped an arm around her and pulled her close. He ran is hand tenderly up and down her bare arm after she released a contented sigh and wrapped her leg around his. He stared up at the ceiling, lost in thought, as his satiated body relaxed.

They had stayed in the bath until the chill of the water drove them out. Mike hoped the warm water would soothe any soreness Marina might feel while giving him time to regain control of his trembling body.

He swore he'd seen fireworks going off in his head when they made love. For someone as inexperienced as Marina, she had to be the sexiest woman he ever met. She hadn't frozen or resisted any of his touches. Her trust was a precious gift he didn't want her ever to regret giving him.

Having his share of lovers over the years—especially through his teens to his late twenties—none had touched his heart the way Marina did.

The last few years had been different. He realized that he'd moved from the stage in his life where he was just seeking mindless pleasure to wanting something deeper. Restless, he hadn't known what he was looking for until he met Marina.

"I love you, Marina," he murmured, turning his head and pressing a kiss to her forehead.

His arms tightened around her when she briefly stiffened. He waited. This was new and very unfamiliar territory for him. He had never told a woman that he loved her before.

"I love you as well, Mike," she said, tilting her head back. He could see the happiness in her eyes. "Together, we make strong magic."

Mike chuckled. "Give me a couple of hours, and I'll show you just how much we can make," he teased, relaxing against the pillows.

A smile lifted the corners of his lips even as his eyelids drooped in exhaustion. His body was still humming from his release and the feel of the woman in his arms. He would give them both a few hours to recoup before he woke her.

We both have a lot more exploring to do, he thought, falling into a deep, restful sleep.

~

Marina smiled in the darkness and snuggled closer to Mike's warm body. His arms held her close against him even as she felt his body relax when he fell asleep. Tilting her head, she studied his strong face. She raised her hand and traced the faint lines near the corner of his mouth with her fingers. His lips parted, and he released a sigh in his sleep.

She decided he had a strong face. His skin was tanned from the sun like hers, and he had thick, dark brown hair. His vivid-blue eyes reminded her of the sky on a clear day. There was a slight bump in the center of his nose, as if it had been broken at one time, and a scar near his upper lip that was so faint, she just noticed it.

With her fingers, she traced the rough beginnings of a beard forming along his jaw. She couldn't help remembering her conversations with her grandmother as she studied him. She had thought her grandmother was joking when the old woman had told her about what it was like to pleasure a man and to be pleasured by one. Her mother had brushed over details, blushing and stammering as she tried to explain. There had been a lot of stuttering, humming, and sighs.

Her father's mother, Ladonna, on the other hand, had cackled and shared fantastic stories with Marina about her different lovers and who had been the best of the best. Her grandmother had gone into so much detail that Marina didn't know if she should believe half of what Ladonna was saying or not. By the end, Marina had seriously decided she might live the rest of her life as a hermit in the Elder forest caring for the trees. It sounded safer.

A small part of her was thankful she had never known her father's father. She didn't think she would ever have been able to look the man in the eye if she had. From the sound of it, the only reason her grandmother knew which one of her lovers had been her grandfather was because of the timing between her affairs.

After her grandfather's untimely departure, her grandmother had explored the kingdoms—and beyond, according to her—in search of new adventures. If that hadn't been more information than Marina wanted to know, her grandmother had given her books to read that she said were retrieved from a distant world.

"They are called romances," Ladonna had chuckled. "They make you wet."

Marina had been very naïve at eighteen summers. She had always been more interested in talking to the trees than talking to the boys in the village. Ladonna had handed her six of these books and told her to read them.

"I cast a spell to translate them. These are my favorites, so be sure to bring them back. And don't let your brothers read them!" Ladonna had instructed her.

Marina had taken the books. She had shaken them, opened them, and inspected them, but for the life of her couldn't figure out how they were supposed to make her wet. Then, she had read one—and understood. By the sixth book, she had learned how to take care of not only the wetness they caused, but the uncomfortable ache they left her feeling after devouring them. Until Mike, she had never had the desire to allow anyone else to take care of the uncomfortable feelings that left her restless and moody. Now, she not only understood what those women in the books were feeling, but she never wanted it to end.

As long as it is with Mike, she thought as she rested her hand over his heart and closed her eyes.

CHAPTER SIXTEEN

Early the next morning, Mike and Marina stood on the front entry steps to the palace. Mike kept his arm wrapped protectively around Marina. After last night, he knew that she belonged to him just as he belonged to her.

It was more than the lovemaking. Their connection had melded them on a level that he never realized was possible. It was as if the two of them had become one—thinking, feeling, and working in unison. He couldn't help wondering if his mom and dad had felt this same kind of connection during their many years of marriage. It was strange how he could suddenly remember them finishing each other's sentences, knowing when the other needed something, and the aching loneliness they felt when they were apart.

He briefly glanced at Orion and Jenny where they stood waiting, along with their two sons, Dolph and Juno. Orion had his arm wrapped around Jenny's waist. After talking with Jenny and seeing how happy she was, he felt confident that whatever brought her here, whether it was the Sea Witch or fate, it was the right thing. Turning his gaze away, he looked around and frowned when he noticed everyone was looking up at the sky.

"Are you sure they're coming?" Mike asked.

"They'll come," Orion replied with confidence.

"I hope they bring DJ and Stone," Juno said, barely containing his excitement as he waited.

Mike leaned toward Marina so he could speak close to her ear. "Why do all the adults seem a bit tense?" he murmured.

"Each ruler is extremely powerful in their own way. Many years ago, there was a great war that divided our kingdoms and pitted one against the other. It was later learned that the war was instigated by the Sea Witch," Marina explained.

Mike fought the urge to roll his eyes. "Why am I not surprised?" he muttered.

"You should not be surprised by anything my cousin does," Orion stated. "She turned all of the dragons to stone." He grimaced when he heard a loud, ground-shaking roar. "Except, of course, for Drago, the King of the Dragons. I don't know why he insists on making a dramatic entrance every time they arrive," Orion added with a shake of his head.

Mike's eyes widened, and he took a step back. His hand pulled free of Marina's, and he automatically began to reach for the gun under his jacket. Marina placed her hand on his arm and shook her head.

"I've only seen the King of the Dragons from afar at the palace when I was visiting Isha," she breathed in awe.

The first thing Mike saw was a swarm of unusual white birds. They swept over the wall of the palace and through the front entrance. He watched as they wove through the guards before spiraling upward.

A moment later, a dark shadow appeared overhead. Mike's eyes followed the huge dragon as it circled the courtyard. The creature's midnight black scales shone brightly in the early morning light. The dragon snapped at a few of Orion's guards as he swooped down. The guards ducked, but didn't move until Kapian called out an order to give Drago more room.

"What is that on his back?" Mike asked, trying to make out the wiggling movements.

"Alright! They came!" Dolph exclaimed.

Mike watched as the two boys standing next to Jenny darted down to the bottom of the steps to wait in excitement. He looked back up at the sky. Drago circled once more before he landed in the center of the courtyard.

The large dragon turned in a tight circle, snapping and snarling at the guards closest to him before he stopped and lowered his right wing. The heads of two small dragons popped up from between his wings. Mike watched in awe as they slid down the wing to the ground and shifted into two boys slightly younger than Juno. All four boys laughed and ran toward each other.

The male dragon turned his gaze to the sky. Mike followed his gaze. A smaller dragon appeared, protected on all sides by the swarm of birds. She swept down over the wall, wobbling a little and barely missing the top. Two guards had to dive to the side to keep from being knocked off. Drago snorted and shook his head. Mike heard Orion chuckle.

"I see she hasn't improved much," Orion said.

"Orion," Jenny chided. "Carly was never graceful when she walked. I can't imagine how hard flying must be, especially carrying little Roo."

It took a moment for Mike to remember what Jenny had told him about Carly being able to turn into a dragon. His gaze moved to the small dragon clutched against the dragon's chest. This one was smaller than the first two who had been on Drago's back. Even from where he was standing, Mike could see two pink bows attached to the pair of tiny horns on her head.

"Bows?" Mike chuckled, amazed by the sight.

"She is adorable!" Marina breathed out in delight.

Mike glanced at Marina's grinning face before turning back to the dragon who was landing beside Drago. A swift shaft of desire to see Marina holding their child struck him hard. The image shook him.

Since when have I ever thought of having kids? he thought in surprise.

He took a quick breath when he saw the dragon shimmer before changing to a woman whose face he had only seen in photographs. He took a step forward, then another two, stopping three steps down when he was positive that the woman was really who he thought she was.

"Carly Tate!" he exclaimed.

Carly turned to look up at him in surprise when she heard her name. Unfortunately, so did the large male dragon. His head whipped around and he took a step toward Mike. The dragon bared his teeth and moved his body in front of Carly and the little dragon she was holding.

"Drago!" Orion warned, stepping down a step and positioning himself between Drago and Mike.

"Who is he, and how does he know my mate?" Drago demanded with a snarl.

"He is from Carly and Jenny's world. He has been searching for them," Orion said.

Drago's lips curled and a long, rumbling growl of warning reverberated through the air. Mike's fingers twitched. He'd feel a hell of a lot better if he had his gun out—though he wasn't sure it would be very effective.

"Well, he found her. Now, he can return to his world. If he tries to take my Carly, I'll kill him," Drago ordered.

A small, strained chuckle escaped Mike at the familiar threat, and he shook his head. "That is a pretty common theme around here," he commented, looking directly into Drago's glowing eyes. "I'll tell you the same thing I told Orion. My job is to make sure that the missing women—in this case, Carly Tate and Jenny Ackerly—were found and are safe. If they want to return to our world, that is entirely up to them. I just need to know they are not being held against their will or need help."

Drago shifted. Mike decided the tall, broad man with the long black hair and piercing golden eyes, which had the flicker of flames dancing in them, was just as much of a threat as the damn dragon! Staring unblinkingly back at the man, he waited for the man to respond.

"You're the cop that Jenny told me about! I'm Carly," the woman said, holding out the dragon in her arms to Drago as she passed him.

"Carly…," Drago said in exasperation, taking his daughter.

"Detective…," Mike corrected with a reassuring smile. "Ms. Tate, it is good to see that you are alive and—well, alive."

Carly laughed. "I don't know about that. Little Roo is teething. We thought she had a cold, but we discovered another tooth last night when she bit Drago. When Drago got the invitation to come, there was no way I was staying behind," she said.

"I wouldn't have left you alone anyway," Drago replied. "Did you forget that you were supposed to stay behind me until I ensured everything was safe?"

Carly rolled her eyes at Drago. "Of course it's safe! We've been here dozens of times, and do you see a lack of guards anywhere?" she demanded with a wave of her hand.

Drago started to growl, but the sound died when the little dragon in his arms grabbed his hand between her front claws and began chewing on his finger. The growl turned into a wince. He pulled his finger free and inspected it.

"No bite, Jen," Drago said.

"*Grrr.* I no Jen, I Roo now," the tiny dragon growled before showing off her shiny new tooth.

Carly shook her head. "We've been calling her by her middle name ever since I discovered Jenny was here. It saves us from the confusion, and she loves it," she said.

Jenny laughed. "Why don't we take the boys to the playroom? Dolph and Juno are thrilled that the boys are back, and Roo can play with Lucy after I feed her," she offered.

"Food!" Roo demanded, suddenly shifting to a chubby little girl with wide golden eyes.

"We will wait for the others to arrive," Orion said with a nod.

"Others? Is Uncle Ashure coming?" Stone asked with a hopeful look.

"He is not your uncle," Drago began before Carly elbowed him, and he grunted. "Well, he isn't. Ashure isn't even a dragon."

Mike pursed his lips together when he saw Drago grimace and a stubborn expression settled on his face. It appeared that Carly Tate was not in the least bit intimidated by the large man. Drago handed Roo to Carly when she held out her hands.

"He's a pirate!" DJ, Drago's oldest son, exclaimed, pulling a wooden sword from his side. "Attack, mates!"

"Come on, you scurvy dogs," Carly ordered before she leaned up and brushed a kiss across Drago's lips. "Be nice to Ashure."

Mike turned and stepped aside to allow Carly, Roo, and the group of boys, who were now planning their creation of a pirate ship, into the playroom behind him. The excited chatter quickly died away as Jenny, Carly, and the children disappeared inside. Slowly walking up the steps to stand next to Marina, Mike once again felt like he had awakened in the matrix of a bizarre world.

"I don't know why the boys think being a pirate is better than being a dragon," Drago muttered.

"Dolph and Juno think the same thing," Orion admitted.

"I could turn him into a burnt pirate with one breath," Drago stated.

"Well, don't. For some unknown reason, both Jenny and Carly like the man," Orion said with a long sigh. "Speaking of which, he has arrived."

Mike watched the arrival of a large carriage being pulled by a dozen horse-like creatures that would make a Clydesdale back home look like a Shetland pony. The creatures were blue with black strips. Their red eyes flashed as they tossed their heads. Ornate silver armor covered their foreheads and chests.

"Is that fire coming out of their nostrils?" Mike asked.

"Nali's going to kill him," Drago and Orion said at the exact same time.

"Nali?" Mike repeated.

Mike swallowed when he felt the hair on the back of his neck suddenly stand up. He swore he could feel the electricity in the air. The thought had no sooner flashed through his mind when he heard the rumbling of thunder. Looking up from the fire-breathing horses, he frowned when all he saw were blue skies.

"I've only heard about her and the mythical Thunderbirds that power her ships," Marina murmured.

Mike could feel his jaw slowly open wide as a futuristic ship came into view. There were four massive birds on each corner of the ship. Threads of electricity ran through their wings, snapping and popping. On the bow, holding onto a long rope, a tall, dark-skinned woman wearing a blood-red blouse and black trousers rested one booted foot on the low railing and stared down at them.

"Holy shi…," Mike started to say when she dove off the flying ship almost a hundred feet in the air.

Long wings suddenly appeared from her back, and she soared downward. She pulled up just before she reached the carriage and landed on the roof. The wings on her back folded and disappeared as she knelt on one knee and braced her hand against the carriage roof.

"I'm going to love watching this. I bet half a gold piece that Nali wins!" Drago said, rubbing his hands together.

"Who is that?" Marina asked, shielding her eyes and looking back up at the ship when a rope dropped down.

"Koorgan,"Orion replied.

"He's a huge son-of-a-bitch," Mike muttered.

"He should be. He's the King of the Giants," Drago replied.

"Only Nali could talk that hard-headed giant off his Isle," Orion commented.

"He refused to help us when the Queen sent a missive," Marina bitterly retorted.

Mike threaded his fingers through Marina's and squeezed her hand in reassurance. The man looked down and waved his hand to a group of guards. Kapian turned and shouted out an order. The guards quickly retreated, clearing an area about the size of a basketball court.

"What's he doing?" Mike asked.

Orion pursed his lips. "Ruining my courtyard," he retorted.

Mike frowned at Orion and looked back up. His breath caught when the man casually stepped off the flying ship. A fall from that height would kill a normal man. The protest that started on his lips once again faded when the man began to grow and grow and grow and grow....

"Brace yourselves," Orion said.

Mike wrapped his arm around Marina and pulled her tightly against his body. The tall man had grown into a giant that stood close to sixty feet tall. The man bent his knees as his feet finally touched the ground. Mike expected the impact to create a thunderous quake. The ground did tremble, but it was more of the rolling effect of a 3.0 quake instead of the catastrophe he was expecting.

Koorgan stood up and grinned. Nali rose to her feet on the roof of the carriage and placed her hands on her hips while another elegantly dressed man leaned out of the carriage and clapped his hands in applause.

"Bravo, Koorgan, bravo. Splendid entrance, my friend," the man in the carriage called from the window.

Koorgan's laugh sounded like thunder. The fire-breathing horses danced and nervously kicked their prancing hooves. Mike watched as Nali snapped her fingers, and the horses instantly settled down.

"Nali, my beautiful Empress. I can explain...," the man warily began, twisting around to look up at the woman standing on the roof of his carriage.

"I swear Ashure, I should slit your thieving throat and be done with it," Nali threatened.

"She won't," Orion assured Mike.

Drago glanced over his shoulder. "I'd almost pay a gold piece to see that," he said, refocusing his attention on the scene in front of him.

"Would that be dragon's gold or sea gold?" Ashure asked.

Mike shook his head while Marina giggled at the antics between the different rulers. He was too fascinated watching the giant Koorgan shrink down to a large man and Nali's graceful flip off the roof to pay attention to anything else. Ashure grimaced and held out his hands when Nali pulled open the door to the carriage and shook her finger at him in a scolding manner.

"I was bringing them to you, Nali. I stole them off a ship heading to the edges of our world. The poor things were in dire condition, and I've...," Ashure's voice died when Nali pinned him to the side of his carriage with one hand.

"You are lucky that I love the brandy that you have, Ashure. Two cases —delivered within the week," she demanded.

"Two bottles and a reward for saving your stallions from the clutches of scoundrels who would have harmed such magnificent beasts," Ashure countered.

Nali gave Ashure a suspicious look before she released him. "One case and I won't charge you for the use of my stallions," she said, releasing him.

"Dapier," Ashure called.

"Aye, your Majesty," Dapier replied.

Mike could appreciate how Ashure casually adjusted the sleeves of his dark brown jacket. The man was cool and calm considering that a woman with wings had just held him up by the neck with one hand. Mike decided that he would have to be very cautious about who he pissed off here. If they didn't burn you to a crisp or step on you, they could rip you apart with one hand.

"Please unload my luggage, return the carriage to my ship, and inform Captain LaBluff to have three bottles of my finest brandy delivered to...." He paused and raised an eyebrow at Nali.

"I'll send several of my Cyclops to retrieve the stallions and the 'case' of brandy," she said.

"You are killing me, Nali," Ashure groaned.

"Aye, your Majesty. The stallions and a case of your finest brandy," Dapier replied, climbing down.

CHAPTER SEVENTEEN

Marina stood near the wall in the large room. Orion had escorted the group into the room after determining that no one else would be arriving. Nali had shaken her head when Orion had quietly asked if she had been in contact with the King and Queen of the Elementals.

"No. Either they have shrouded their Isle or something else has happened. I was unable to locate it," Nali explained.

"I told you Ruger had floated his kingdom away," Ashure said, wiggling his fingers.

Marina giggled and leaned close to Mike. "I like him. He is funny," she murmured.

"He's a pirate," Mike retorted with a shake of his head. "Talk about stereotyping! He could be straight out of the movies. The only difference is, he is a lot cleaner."

Marina bit her lip when the Pirate King turned and winked at her. She squeezed Mike's hand when he shot Ashure a warning look. Mike turned to gaze down at her with a wry grin.

"Another new experience for me," he confessed.

"What is that?" she asked, tilting her head to look up at him.

"Jealousy," he murmured.

Marina drew in a swift breath when he bent and captured her lips in a possessive kiss. She turned into him and threaded her fingers through his hair while returning his kiss.

"Looks like you missed another one, Ashure," Nali commented.

Ashure grinned. "It is the history of my life. I find an enchanting woman, and she is already taken—except for you, my beautiful Empress," he retorted with a wicked smile.

"Oh, Goddess help me," Nali groaned, turning to look at Orion and Drago. "Please—tell me where I can find a woman who would put up with this thief."

Koorgan laughed. "Is there such a woman?" he asked.

Ashure gave the group a pained look and walked over to the bar. He picked up several bottles and examined them before he chose one and walked back to the table with it. Pulling off the glass stopper, he poured himself a glass before sitting down.

"I believe we were asked to attend a meeting here for something more serious," he prompted with a lift of his glass toward Orion. "I would hate to come all this way just to lose my fire beasts and an excellent case of brandy."

Orion nodded in response, turned, and signaled Marina and Mike to step forward. Each ruler settled down around the table. Drago leaned over, grabbed the bottle of liquor in front of Ashure, and poured two glasses. He then pushed them toward Marina and Mike.

"Marina, please explain to the others what you have shared with me," Orion encouraged, waving for them to sit down.

Mike pulled out a chair for Marina. She gave him a grateful smile before sitting down and nervously wrapping her hands around the glass of amber liquid. She took a deep breath and released it before slowly studying the face of each person at the table.

"My name is Marina Fae. I am a witch from the Isle of Magic, and I have come to beg for your help," she began.

Over the next half hour, she shared everything that had happened to her people and herself. Mike reached over and gripped her hand as she impatiently wiped a tear that coursed down her cheek as she told them about what happened to Geoff and the sacrifice her grandmother had made for them to be there.

"Please help us. King Drago, you know what it feels like to lose those you care about. She is slowly killing my people the way she killed yours," Marina forced out in a trembling voice.

A muscle ticked in Drago's jaw. His expression was hard and his eyes cold. Marina wasn't sure if she should have mentioned the loss of Drago's people, but she wanted him to understand the hopelessness she was feeling.

Drago turned to look at Orion. "I'm going to kill that bitch," he announced.

"Drago… remember what I told you before," Nali cautioned.

Drago slammed his fist into the table. The wood snapped under the force. A long crack appeared and the glasses and bottle of liquor began to slide toward the center when the table started to cave in. Marina splayed her hands over the wood and spoke to it. Her magic flowed through her, healing the fractured wood. Each of the rulers had risen when the table began to collapse. Mike laid his hand on her back. A surge of magical power flowed through her, stronger with his light touch even though her magic was not impeded on this kingdom.

"I love the power of magic," Ashure replied with a sigh.

Marina blinked and glanced around those standing by the table. "My powers are mostly with wood," she said.

Orion scowled at Drago. "The next time there is a meeting, we are having it on the Isle of the Dragons. Between Koorgan putting giant footprints in my courtyard and you almost breaking a thousand year old table, I'm about ready to ban you both from my home," he snapped.

"What about Ashure?" Koorgan said with a raised eyebrow.

"What have I done?" Ashure demanded, glaring at Koorgan.

"The silver dagger on the tray," Koorgan chuckled.

Ashure grimaced and pulled the silver dagger, which he had picked up off of a tray sitting on the meeting room bar, from his pocket. He balanced it on his finger for a moment before twirling it and placing it on the table. A crooked grin curved his lips at Orion's exasperated expression.

"I wouldn't have kept it," Ashure retorted.

"Boys! I swear none of you have grown up since I first met you as children," Nali said with a shake of her head before she turned to look at Marina. "I will help you free your people. The black evil inside the Sea Witch has been spreading out to seek other hosts. We must stop it before it is successful."

"You keep saying there is something inside Magna. The only thing I saw was her black heart," Drago snarled. "I say I kill her and cut her heart out of her chest."

"Dragons have always been bloodthirsty beasts," Ashure commented.

Drago turned, his eyes dancing with flames, and gave Ashure a menacing grin. "How about I show you firsthand how bloodthirsty I can be?" he offered.

Ashure's gaze hardened, and his mouth tightened. Marina's eyes widened when she saw the flare of magic surrounding Ashure. His aura, which had been faint but light and colorful, suddenly turned to a thick and menacing black, unlike anything she had ever seen before—even Magna. The coldness threatened to choke her. When the swirling color turned toward her, as if aware that she could see it, she saw faces and greedy hands reaching for her. Frightened, she released a startled cry and swiftly rose from her chair, reaching for Mike as she jerked away.

"Marina, what is it?" Nali asked in concern.

Marina's terrified gaze locked with Ashure's. The Pirate King's expression changed. He took a deep breath. There was a look of warning for Marina to keep what she saw to herself. Her head unconsciously rose and fell in a short, jerky nod. She held onto Mike, her body trembling, even as the tortured faces locked in Ashure's aura faded.

"I… Nothing…," she whispered, tearing her gaze away from Ashure. "Please… I need a moment alone."

"Marina," Mike said, watching her turn and hurry out of the room.

Marina shook her head. She needed a few minutes alone to compose herself. There were stories told as she was growing up that the Kings and Queens of the Isles were not what they appeared to be. She had learned today that the stories were true, but some of them were vastly understated.

The sound of the door quietly closing behind Marina echoed loudly in the suddenly silent room. Mike turned and gave each person in the room a cold, hard look of warning. Stepping up to the table, he braced his hands on it and spoke in a slow, measured cadence.

"I don't give a fuck what you are," he started, capturing each person's gaze again. "I don't give a damn if you have issues with each other. What I do care about is what is happening to Marina and her people. My job is to serve and protect. I will do that. It is not to go in with the intention of revenge. It is to go in with the intention of freeing those imprisoned by this Sea Witch. I don't know if the spell she created will affect you the way it does Magna and the others with magic. If it does, you can expect to feel weak. Now, are you going to work with us or not?"

"I have said I will. The spell will affect each of us. I will have to keep my ogres away, but the Cyclops and Minotaurs who are members of my crew should be safe," Nali said.

"You get me. There are no other dragons who can fight, but *I* will fight —and try not to kill her if I can," Drago responded.

"I will fight as well. I should have taken care of her long ago," Orion said.

Koorgan nodded. "I should have come to Queen Magika when she first asked," he replied with a sigh of regret. "I will stand with you."

Mike's gaze moved to Ashure. The man's troubled expression cleared, and he nodded. Mike didn't miss the way Ashure's gaze kept going to the door that Marina had escaped through.

"A pirate never turns down a good fight," he replied in a light tone that belied the steely look in his eyes. "Of course we will fight."

Mike nodded and gave everyone a grim smile. "Does anyone have a map of the Isle, specifically the palace?" he asked with a raised eyebrow.

"I do," Marina quietly said, stepping back into the room.

Mike turned and saw that her expression was determined even if her eyes were slightly red. She lifted her chin and returned his gaze. She had retrieved Mr. Bow from their room. Lifting his arm, he held out his hand to her.

"Are you alright?" he murmured under his breath.

Marina nodded as she grasped his hand and squeezed his fingers. He noticed that she kept her gaze focused on Ashure.

"Thank you for helping my people," Marina finally said.

"Now, this is what we will do…," Orion began.

CHAPTER EIGHTEEN

"You are a very unusual woman, Marina Fae of the Isle of Magic," Ashure casually commented later that evening.

Marina lifted her chin and turned at the sound of Ashure's voice. Her back was pressed against the stone balcony railing. Behind her, the beautiful palace gardens were coming alive with twinkling lights as the night blooming flowers opened up to catch the moon beams shining down from the nearly full moon.

She had stepped outside to revel in the beauty of the night and the fact that she didn't feel drained by Magna's horrible spell. It seemed a lifetime since she had been able to enjoy the daytime, much less the suffocating tiredness of nightfall. Mike was still inside, talking with Carly and Jenny. She had quietly slipped away, afraid that he would talk about returning to his world.

Marina studied Ashure's aura. It was once again the faint yet colorful hue that was nonthreatening. In the background, she could hear the others quietly talking. The open door and voices reassured her that she wasn't alone. Still, she couldn't quite keep her fingers from itching to call for Mr. Bow. Her gaze moved to where he was hanging near the door to the dining room.

"I am but a simple witch, your Majesty," Marina replied, turning back to stare out at the garden.

"Not so simple, I would argue," he said, coming to stand next to her.

He reached out and gripped the railing. His gaze moved over the garden, watching as the flowers lit up in a wide, vivid display of color. He took a deep breath.

"I don't know what you mean," she lied.

Ashure chuckled and glanced at her before returning his attention to the garden. "You should never lie to a pirate, my dear. We are gifted with the ability to smell a lie," he said, briefly touching his nose with one finger.

"I may have certain talents," she finally admitted.

"Powerful ones that are very dangerous to some people," he murmured with a slight thread of steel in his voice.

Marina didn't reply. While his words might have sounded threatening, neither his aura, which she could see out of the corner of her eye, or his tone made her feel as if he was a danger to her. Still, she could not erase the memory of tortured faces and beseeching hands reaching for her.

"How… How can you stand it?" she wondered aloud, unsure of how to finish her question.

Ashure dryly chuckled. "We are not always given a choice as to what happens to us in our lives. It is how we deal with what we are given that defines who we are and who we are to become," he replied.

Marina thought about what Ashure had said. For a man who liked to appear light-hearted and unconcerned, his response was perceptive. She could appreciate his insight. Growing up, she had thought of her ability to see other people's magic as a burden.

"Grandmother warned me to make sure that the evil inside Magna does not touch the Keeper of Lost Souls. You are the Keeper, aren't you?" she quietly asked, turning her head to look at Ashure's face.

His face hardened for a moment before he relaxed. "I am many things, Marina. Some might call me a keeper. Some accuse me of keeping them prisoner—while others call me a thief," he replied with a shrug.

"What would you call yourself?" she asked, unable to contain her curiosity.

Ashure flashed her a brief smile. "All of the above and a great lover," he replied. He said the last part slightly louder and turned at the same time. Marina stood still when he grabbed her hand and pressed a kiss to the back of it before releasing it. "If you ever tire of your human, I would be happy to console you should you need a diversion, my powerful and noble witch."

Marina blinked in surprise and pulled her hand away. Ashure nodded to Mike and murmured that it was a beautiful night before disappearing back inside. Her gaze followed the Pirate King. He was a very complex man under his elegant coat.

"What was all that about?" Mike asked, following her gaze.

"Accepting the gifts we have been given by the Goddess, even if they feel more like a curse," she replied in a distracted voice.

Alone later that evening, Marina sat at the dressing table brushing her hair. Placing the brush on the table, she divided her hair into four sections and began braiding it. In the mirror, she could see Mike sitting on the end of their bed, inspecting the weapon from his world.

"What will you do if we survive this?" she quietly asked, tying off the end of her hair and letting her hands fall to her lap.

Mike looked up at her and frowned. He shook his head and smiled. His gaze was deadly serious when he answered her.

"Not if, *when* we free your people, I'm not sure. I honestly haven't thought that far with everything going on," he confessed, rising off the bed and replacing his weapon in the leather holster.

"Will you return to your world?" she asked.

Mike's expression grew thoughtful. She could see that he wasn't sure how to answer her. Turning on the seat, she rose and walked toward him. Doubt grew inside her at his continued silence.

"Marina...," he started to say.

She stopped in front of him and searched his eyes, seeing the frustration and indecision in them. Biting her lip, she placed her hand on his chest over his heart.

"You know that I love you, and I know that you love me, but is our love enough that you would stay in my world?" she asked, fingering the buttons on his shirt.

Mike captured her hand. Bringing it to his lips, he pressed a kiss to her fingertips. Desire pulled at Marina when he reached out with his other hand and slid it along her waist.

"I do care about you. Hell, I more than care—I meant it when I said that I love you," he replied in a rough voice.

Marina slid her arms around his waist and rested her head against his chest. Closing her eyes, she took a deep breath, loving the warmth of his body against hers. Yet, doubt continued to plague her even with his words. If he loved her, why would he hesitate to tell her whether he planned to stay or leave her?

"But—you still plan to return to your world, don't you?" she murmured.

Mike pulled back and raised his hands to cup her face. She returned his steady gaze. There was an intensity to him, a determination that told her that he did plan to leave. A stifled cry of denial slipped out before she could contain it. Pulling away, she shook her head and backed up several feet. Trembling, she fought to control her rising panic.

"I have to go back," he said in a grim tone.

Marina wrapped her arms around her waist. Her eyes burned, but she refused to allow any tears to fall. She would not attempt to hold him to her if he did not wish to be there. Unfortunately, she couldn't hide the distress on her face at his grimly spoken words.

"Then, you should go before we leave," she said in a trembling voice.

Mike blinked in surprise. "What?"

Marina dropped her arms to her side and clenched her hands into tight fists. Lifting her chin, she drew on the strength she had developed over the past year. She would not allow him to see how much this was tearing her apart.

"I said you should leave now. I will ask Orion if he can create a portal so you may return to your world. If he can't, I'm sure that one of the others can. They are very powerful, much more than I. You should not risk your life for people you don't know," she stated.

Mike stared at her like she had lost her mind. Marina didn't care. She would rather he left before there was a chance of something happening to him. At least if he returned to his world, she would know he was safe. There was no need for him to remain anyway. The combined strength of the remaining rulers and their armies were surely strong enough to defeat Magna and her creatures, especially if they attacked before dawn when her magic was weak.

"No," he replied between gritted teeth.

Marina blinked. "What do you mean no? This is not your fight, Mike. You have done enough. There is no need for you to risk your… life." She pursed her lips and shook her head when her voice broke on the last word.

Bowing her head, she closed her eyes. She had to get out of the room. The fragile hold she had on her emotions was quickly dissolving. If she didn't leave now, she would make a fool of herself and beg him to tell her why he didn't want to stay with her if he loved her.

"I plan to come back, Marina," Mike said, taking a step closer to her. "I have to return, but only so that I can say goodbye."

Marina slowly lifted her head and opened her eyes. Tears glittered in them, hanging onto her lower lashes but not falling. Lifting a hand, she brushed it across her pale cheek.

"Goodbye?" she repeated.

Mike's expression softened at her whispered word. He cupped her face again. His eyes searched her face. He must have seen the uncertainty, fear, and despair in her eyes because he bent his head and brushed a rough kiss across her lips. Pulling back, he made sure she understood what he was telling her.

"I told you a little about my life back there and about my sister Ruth. I know she is probably getting frantic. She will tear Yachats State Park apart, stone by stone if I know her. I'm all the family she has, and until I met you, Geoff, and Erin, she was all the family I had—well, except for Charlie, but that is a different story," he muttered.

"I understand. I feel the same way about my parents and brothers," she replied.

"I need to let her know that I'm okay. That—hell, I don't know what I'll tell her; but essentially, I'll let her know she doesn't have to worry about me. I know it isn't safe to take you back with me. I won't risk anything happening to you, but I sure as hell will be coming back. I love you, damn it. I love you."

Marina met his lips when he bent his head to kiss her again. Their breaths came in rough, uneven gasps as the heat inside them built. She pulled away with a gasp when she felt the cool air on her breasts. During their kiss, Mike had been busy undoing the clasps on the forest green blouse Kelia had given her this morning.

"I want you," he said, pressing kisses along her jaw.

A soft moan slipped from her lips when he cupped her breasts in his hands. She frantically fumbled to open his shirt. A groan of frustration resounded through the room when she realized that the buttons only went half way down the front. She would need to pull his shirt over his head to strip it from him.

He reached down, grabbed the bottom of his shirt, and pulled it over his head. His muscles rippled as he tossed it to the side. He deftly removed her blouse and the black bra under it.

"It only seems fair," he teased, cupping her breasts.

Marina lowered her eyelids and moaned as he played with her hardening nipples. "How is it that you affect me like this? I can already feel the warmth between my legs as my body gets ready for you," she confessed.

Mike paused for a brief second before he cursed. "Damn, woman, you say the sexiest things," he said in a deep voice.

"Sexy?" she repeated.

Bending forward, he began undoing her pants when she didn't move fast enough. "You make me wish that I brought my handcuffs. I'd love to tie you up," he muttered, pushing her pants down.

"I do not know what handcuffs are, but would a belt work?" she asked, glancing over at the robe lying across the back of the chair.

Mike froze. He didn't mean to say that out loud. He'd planned to work his way up to some of the more risqué ways of making love after he felt confident that Marina was ready. He wasn't into the hardcore bondage stuff, but he wasn't opposed to having a little fun in the bedroom.

He followed her gaze and saw what she was talking about. Heat flared inside him, and he knew that this time was going to be fast, dirty, and very pleasurable. Bending, he swept her off her feet.

"Mike!"

He gave her a fierce glance before he strode over to the bed. He was thankful that the covers were already turned down for the night.

Placing a knee on the bed, he gently laid her down on the light blue linens.

"Stay like that," he ordered in a soft, firm voice.

Marina nodded. He could feel her eyes on him as he undressed. Placing his trousers on the chair, he pulled the belt free from the silk robe. He grimaced when he felt his body's immediate reaction.

"Uh, Mike...," Marina called, interrupting his thoughts.

He turned his head to look at her. She remained where he had told her to, but her gaze kept moving toward the table near the balcony doors. He frowned and glanced over. He slowly smiled in understanding and nodded at her silent plea.

Gripping the belt in one hand, he walked over to Mr. Bow where it lay on a small table humming. He picked up the bow and held it in his other hand, turned back, and crossed the room. A low groan escaped the bow.

"I was being good," Mr. Bow complained. "I was minding my own business."

"It doesn't matter. Marina is uncomfortable," Mike chuckled.

"Do you have any idea how long I was around before I was a bow? I've seen things you and Marina could only dream of doing! If you want some advice, I can tell you...."

Mike bent over, placed the bow in the closet, and shut the door, cutting off Mr. Bow's words of wisdom. It would be a cold day in hell before he let a tree tell him how to make love to his woman. He walked back over to the bed.

"Thank you," she said, blushing.

Mike climbed up on the bed and straddled her waist. Her eyes widened when he held out his hand and allowed the belt to unfurl from his fingers. He gave her a wicked smile and motioned for her to lift her arms.

"You can thank me afterwards," he informed her.

If he thought she would be intimidated, he was wrong. Instead, she lifted her wrists up and rolled her hips under his buttocks. Leaning forward, he caught her wrists and wrapped the silk around them. Reaching up, he looped the other end around the headboard of the bed. What he did not anticipate was that the angle would align his cock with her lips.

The moment he felt her warm breath and moist tongue against the tip of his cock he knew he had lost control of the situation. His plans to tease her, make her come, and tease her again dissolved into mindless pleasure when she suddenly wrapped her lips around the end of his cock, rose her head up, and slid it further into her mouth.

He gripped the headboard of the bed, the end of the belt still in his hands and looked down. Marina was beautiful as she sucked on him. He moved His hips back and forth in unison. Reaching down next to her, he pulled a pillow up under her head.

He curled his fingers as he slowly slid his cock back and forth. The mesmerizing feel and sight of her lips around him were captivating. He finished tying off the belt so her arms were above her head. Once he was finished, he lowered his hands behind his back and found her swollen nub.

She moaned around his cock, and he swore the vibration traveled in a direct line to his balls. Realizing he was very close to coming, he pulled free. Her soft words of protest echoed through the room. He ignored them as he slid down her body and between her legs.

"Mike," she whimpered, twisting against the covers.

The belt was loose enough that she could pull her hands free if she wanted, but she didn't. Instead, she gripped the strap, her body arching in need. Lifting her legs, he placed one over each of his shoulders, pressing a kiss to the inside of each one as he did it.

Her body arched again, lifting her soft curls up to him in invitation even as her heels pressed against his back. Spreading her folds, he bent forward and caught the small nub between his lips and began sucking. She stiffened, her back arched and her head thrown back as her hands twisted and fought to control the intense pleasure engulfing her.

"Come for me, baby," he murmured, teasing her clit with his tongue. "Come all over my mouth."

Marina's loud pants increased. Her breasts swayed, and her body trembled as he increased his attack on her core with a combination of finger fucking, licks, and hard sucking. Her lips parted and she turned her face into her arm, releasing a scream as she came hard.

Mike lapped up her release, coaxing from her a series of mini orgasms. He could feel her channel squeezing his fingers. The need to feel that same tightness around his cock drove him to his knees. Her legs slipped off his shoulders, and he caught them in his arms as he prepared to enter her.

Still trapped in the aftermath of her orgasm, Mike thrust his cock as deep as he could before pulling out and doing it again and again. He kept her legs trapped in his arms, her hips raised, and his gaze locked on the mindless ecstasy that she was experiencing.

He could feel the change in her body when she realized that he wasn't finished with her yet. Marina was struggling to release her wrists, but she ended up twisting them tighter. Mike rocked his hips forward harder and deeper with each thrust as his fragile control snapped.

Marina's body began to glow with the colors of her magic. Mike could feel the tingling of her aura against his skin, wrapping around him. He fell forward when she finally released her wrists and reached for him. Wrapping her legs around his hips as he leaned over her, she pulled his head down and captured his lips. The combined taste of their love-making mixed on their breath as they kissed.

Mike could feel his release build to a breaking point. Sliding his arms underneath her, he drove his hips hard enough that the massive bed shook. He broke their kiss and buried his face in her neck as he came. He shook from the force and fought to catch his breath. Every muscle strained to hold Marina closer and bury himself deeper inside her.

Their hips ground together as his cock pulsed his seed deep into her womb.

They lay like that, still connected to each other, his face buried against her neck. In all honesty, he didn't think he could have pulled free of her. His cock was still massively hard and thick and her canal held him in a tight fist.

Breathing heavily, he pressed kisses to her passion-damp skin. Unable to resist, he nipped at her neck. He wanted to leave his mark on her.

"You make me want to do crazy things," he finally murmured.

"Mm… Like what?" she asked in a sleepy voice.

He pulled back and gazed down at her with a serious expression. "Like asking you to be my wife," he said.

Marina turned her head and gazed up at him. The sleepy, satiated look faded and her eyes cleared. He could see her confusion.

"What are you saying, Mike?" she asked.

Mike brushed a kiss across her lips before leaning his weight onto his right side and reaching for her hand. He brought it to his lips and pressed a kiss to her fingers.

"Marina Fae of the Isle of Magic, I'm asking if you would do me the pleasure of becoming my wife," he repeated.

Marina's eyes shimmered with tears before she gave him a trembling smile. "Yes, Mike Hallbrook. My answer is yes," she whispered before pulling his head down and capturing his lips again.

CHAPTER NINETEEN

By the next afternoon, the palace courtyard on the Isle of the Sea Serpent looked like a staging area for a massive attack force. Mike had never seen such a mixture of warriors in his life. He couldn't imagine how the war between each of these species must have played out. Hell, even with only one dragon, it was enough to scare the shit out of him.

He glanced up at the sky. A dozen of Nali's airships, complete with the thunderbirds, hovered above them. Earlier, he had seen the same number of pirate ships. Nearly a hundred giants appeared, arriving on great flying beasts that looked suspiciously like the hippogriffs he used to draw when he was a kid.

"This is incredible," Marina breathed, coming to stand next to him on the front steps.

"I have to agree," he replied with a grin.

Mike watched as Marina hugged Mr. Bow to her chest. He could feel her nervousness and her excitement for her people. He reached over and ran his hand down along her back in comfort.

"Surely with this much force, the Sea Witch can be defeated," she added, nervously biting her bottom lip.

"We will not stop until your people are free, Marina," Orion promised, coming to stand next to them.

"How badly will Magna's spell affect everyone?" Mike asked.

"It is possible it will affect some of us more than others. We have planned the attack so that our powers are minimally impacted if the spell does affect us strongly. We do not plan to give Magna time to utilize her magic," Orion explained.

"Everyone is ready. Of my people, I could possibly be the only one affected by Magna's spell. My monsters will protect me until dawn if that is the case," Nali said, climbing the steps.

"I will remain in my dragon form. The spell should not affect me as much then," Drago replied.

Mike watched warily as Ashure came up the steps two at a time. Ashure nodded to the others before he turned his gaze to Mike and Marina. Mike pulled Marina closer to his side when the pirate chuckled.

"You are a smart man, my wily human warrior. She is worth keeping a close eye on," Ashure remarked.

"Are your men ready, Ashure?" Drago asked.

"Of course! They live for a good fight—especially one where they will more than likely die or be turned to stone like your unfortunate clan," Ashure replied dryly.

Drago started toward Ashure, but Carly stepped forward and put her hand on Drago's chest. Tugging gently on his beard, she made him look at her instead. Mike watched in amazement as Carly skillfully distracted the giant dragon.

"You'd better not get hurt, or I'm going to take the kids and my paper birds back to Oregon," she threatened in an unsteady voice that broke on the last word.

The rumble of Drago's growl was easily heard by everyone standing nearby. Drago swept Carly into his arms. He scowled at all of them.

"I need to speak with my mate," he said in a gruff tone before he turned and disappeared into the palace.

"I never expected that," Ashure commented with wide eyes.

"Everyone prepare to leave in two hours," Orion said, his gaze locked on where Jenny was pensively standing by one of the pillars.

"I need to speak with my men," Koorgan stated.

"Well, I could use a drink. Ashure, come on. You can pour it," Nali ordered in a tone that said she wanted to have a talk with him.

"What did I do this time?" Ashure asked with a groan that quickly turned to a loud curse when Nali wrapped her arm around his waist. Mike blinked and took a step back when wings suddenly appeared from her back and she pushed up off the ground. "Goddess' fingernails, Nali! You know I hate it when you do this without warning!" Ashure yelled.

Mike shook his head and watched as they disappeared over the side of Nali's airship. Shaking his head, he looked down at Marina. He could see the wonder in her eyes as well.

"I'm glad I'm not the only one who thinks this is crazy," he teased.

"I never thought that royalty could be so entertaining," she confessed with a grin.

"You know, we have a couple of hours that we could kill doing something much more interesting," Mike murmured.

Marina's eyes widened before she gazed at him with a wicked gleam in her eyes. "Can I tie you up this time?" she asked with a suggestive grin.

"Oh, please! Put me in the closet again," Mr. Bow muttered with a sigh.

Two hours later, Marina called out to Mike as he finished pulling on his boots. He felt strange dressed like the locals. The knee-high, dark-brown boots fitted over the form-fitting, matching, brown pants. The taupe-colored shirt and black vest finished off his outfit. He felt like he was dressing up to go find missing treasures. All he needed was a broad-rimmed hat and a whip!

"Mike, it is time to leave," Marina called from the other room.

"I'm ready," he answered, buckling his gun holster around across his chest before picking up his jacket.

"Do you.... Shit, Marina," Mike said, pausing in the doorway between their room and the bathroom.

"What is it?" she asked, turning in a circle and frowning.

Mike pulled his jacket on and walked toward her. He wrapped his arm around her waist and pulled her against him. She tilted her head back and rose up on her toes to kiss him.

"You are so beautiful, and I'm scared to death something might happen to you," he admitted in a slightly uneven voice.

Her gaze softened, and she raised a hand, running it down his cheek. Mike turned his head and pressed a kiss to her palm. He wished there was a way to leave her here with Jenny and Carly.

"They are my people, my family. I have fought to protect them, and I will continue to do so. Erin and the other children are there. I've already been gone too long. What if something has happened to them as well?" she fretted.

"They are smart. You taught them well—just, be careful," he said.

"I will. I promise," she replied.

Her promise didn't completely wipe away Mike's feeling of unease. He was going up against creatures straight out of a horror novel. The memory of the Hellhound he had killed on the beach flashed through his mind. It had only been injured until Marina shot it with her arrows. Now, he had only a few bullets left. Once his clip was empty, he was defenseless against such creatures.

A knock on the door drew their attention to the fact that it was time to leave. Nodding to Marina, he followed her to the door. Marina strapped Mr. Bow to her side, and took a deep breath before she opened the door. Jenny stood on the other side of the door looking pale but composed. She gave them an uneven smile before murmuring that Orion and the others were waiting for them on the front steps.

Following Jenny down the grand corridor, Mike couldn't help but think of the young woman he had met over a year ago. His admiration for her grew when he realized everything she must have gone through after finding herself in this strange world.

"Jenny."

Jenny slowed and glanced over her shoulder at him. They paused a short distance from the open front doors. Mike could see that Jenny was having a hard time keeping her eyes from moving to Orion.

"Yes, Mike," she said, turning to look at him.

"Did you ever have any second thoughts or doubts that you belonged here?" he asked, aware that Marina had stiffened beside him.

Jenny's tense expression softened, and she shook her head. "Never," she said. "Do you?"

Mike shook his head. "No, it is strange, but it feels right to be here," he finally admitted.

"Is everything alright?" Orion asked, stepping through the door to join them.

Mike nodded. "You don't happen to have an extra knife or a bazooka on you, would you?" he half-heartedly joked.

Jenny giggled while Marina and Orion looked at him with a blank expression. Clearing his throat, Mike twisted his lips in sardonic amusement. Obviously they didn't have bazookas in magical realms. Of course, who needed them when you had fire-breathing dragons and scary monsters?

"I could use a knife if you have one to spare," Mike clarified.

"Ah, yes, of course," Orion said with a nod. "Kapian, Mike needs a blade."

"Yes, your Majesty," Kapian said, with a snap of his fingers.

A minute later, Mike was strapping a sword on his hip. He would have made a sarcastic comment that it was overkill, but he felt that, before the night was over, he would be thankful he had it instead of the hunting knife.

"My men are ready. We will arrive by sea as planned," Orion said as Mike secured his sword.

"Are you sure Magna won't know we are coming?" Mike asked, studying the man.

Orion returned Mike's scrutiny with a determined look of his own. "Magna's spell should not affect us as it does those living on the Isle of Magic. Our magic is different and all spells do not work the same. Also, we will not be affected for as long as those on the isle," he explained. "Drago will come in from the air while we approach from the sea. As we planned earlier, Marina and you will meet us on the north beach as it is close to the river and more isolated. There is no reason for any of Magna's creatures to be there since there are no villages along that section of the isle according to Marina."

"We will guide you to the river, King Orion. Drago will patrol the skies until you reach the lake. Nali and her monsters will descend upon the palace from the city. A reminder, King Orion, that the river that runs under the palace walls to the north and comes up on the other side into the lake is very deep and treacherous," Marina warned.

Orion gave a sardonic smile. "For those who cannot breathe underwater," he interjected. "I will take several of my men with me and open the gates for Nali's warriors."

"Will she be able to protect the statues in the garden? She might be weak from Magna's spell," Jenny commented with a frown.

"Nali informed me a short while ago that she has come up with a solution to the issue. She won't be in a form that will be affected by the spell," Orion assured Jenny.

"Inside the palace, King Drago will protect those that she turned to stone and destroy the Hellhounds while Mike and I locate the King and free him," Marina continued, recounting their plans from earlier.

"I will deal with Magna once and for all. We cannot risk her harming the Queen and King." Orion stated.

"It's time to move out. We will see you in three hours," Mike replied with a nod to the others.

"We will meet you in three hours on the north beach," Orion confirmed. "It will be dark and Magna should have retreated to the palace by then."

Mike watched as Orion reached out and pulled Jenny towards him. They held each other for a moment before Orion stepped back. Turning, the Sea King lifted his hand and signaled to the others that it was time to leave.

Mike wrapped his arm around Marina's waist. He tightened his face in resignation when she handed him the colored stones from her grandmother. He gave her a wry smile before he bent over and placed them on the floor. Straightening, he looked at her, glad that they were alone.

"At least I'll have time to get over being sick before everyone else arrives," he said with a rueful expression.

Marina shook her head as she stepped into the circle beside him. "I have an idea," she replied.

Mike started when she wound her arms around his neck. He instinctively moved his hands down to her waste and gripped her hips, pulling her against him. Bending his head until his lips were almost touching hers, he couldn't resist closing the final distance. He pressed a brief, hard kiss to her lips.

"What idea is that? Is it anything like a couple of hours ago?" Mike teased.

Marina sighed. "If only it could be. I'm going to distract you. I don't have to say the chant aloud for it to work," she murmured before she closed her eyes and kissed him again.

Mike's low groan echoed through the room as the swirling colors engulfed them. He closed his eyes, hoping to keep the nausea at bay this time. He could feel the magic flowing around him—through him. He was familiar with the feel of it now and didn't resist the invisible tug as Marina cast her spell. Warmth swept through him, and he swore he could see the silvery threads connecting them together even though his eyes were closed. He deepened their kiss when Marina's lips parted beneath his and her tongue teased him, reminding him of the other pleasures she had given him a short time ago.

As far as I'm concerned, she can distract me any time she wants, he thought as the room around them faded, and he found himself standing on a soft, sandy beach.

Lifting his head, he blinked in disorientation. Moonlight glittered on the water a short distance from where they were standing. To their left, the trees swayed in the breeze as if cheering Marina's return.

"That wasn't so bad," Mike murmured, his eyes quickly adjusting to the darkness. He turned to look down at Marina just as her eyes rolled back in her head. "Marina!"

Mike's arms protectively tightened around Marina when her legs gave out from under her. Her eyes fluttered for a moment as she fought to keep them open, but it was impossible. The weight of Magna's spell had slammed into her, draining all the energy from her body even with Mike's touch.

He picked her up in his arms and carried her over to a nearby tree where he gently lowered her to a soft thatch of grass growing underneath. He unhooked Mr. Bow and laid it to the side before he slid his hand along her cheek and cupped it. His hand trembled slightly as he waited until she opened her eyes. He needed to reassure himself that she was alright.

"It's Magna's spell and the drain from creating the portal. My magic is not made for such spells," she whispered, forcing her eyes open. "Give me a few minutes."

Mike breathed a sigh of relief. "Take all the time you need," he said.

He removed his jacket and placed it over her. Turning, he sat down next to her and gently lifted her head so she could use his lap as a pillow. He tenderly brushed her braid to the side.

Shivering, Marina rolled onto her side and pulled his jacket around her. "I can feel the power within you," she whispered with a sigh. "It is giving me strength. Already, I feel stronger than I would have."

"Take all the power you need, honey," Mike offered, leaning back against the tree and staring out at the ocean. "It is beautiful here."

"One day I would like to show you how beautiful it truly is," Marina murmured in a barely audible voice.

Mike tightened his hold on her slender figure. He could feel her fatigue. The spell took a lot out of her. Before, her grandmother had helped. This time, Marina had used every bit to transport them here.

He leaned over and picked up Mr. Bow, placing it next to her. He smiled when she pulled the bow under the jacket and hugged it close to her. Shifting a little more, he moved until he could straighten his legs. Tilting his head back, he stared up at the stars. Unobstructed, he could see the center of the star system running south to north like a wide river.

"Sleep," he instructed, brushing his hand along her silky hair. "I'll wake you when the others arrive."

Marina started to shake her head before she sighed. "I shouldn't, but I'm so tired," she grumbled

Mike's hand paused. "Get some rest. We will need you to be ready," he ordered in a gruff voice.

She was silent for several seconds. Mike thought she had fallen asleep until she turned her head and brushed a kiss against his leg.

"You are a good man, Mike Hallbrook," she sighed. "I'm glad you are here."

Mike felt his chest tighten at her softly spoken confession. He listened as her breathing grew steady and knew she had fallen asleep. Relaxing, he leaned back against the tree and gazed out at the glittering ocean. The light from the twin moons created millions of dancing diamonds that reflected on the surface of the water. Love and fear warred inside him as he continued to tenderly stroke her hair.

"I'm glad I'm here, too," he whispered, settling down to watch and wait for the others' arrival.

CHAPTER TWENTY

Mike's soft whisper in her ear woke Marina from a sound sleep. She sat up and blinked in surprise, feeling more refreshed than she had in over a year, and…

"It's still dark," she whispered in amazement, turning to look up at Mike with shining eyes. "I don't feel the weight that normally drains me."

Mike's eyes glittered for a moment before he concealed his anger. "It is all the positive mojo I was giving you while you slept," he teased, shifting and rising to his feet.

She took the hand he offered and stood as well. They both stretched. For the first time, Marina could actually see Magna's spell swirling like fine threads through the air. The threads recoiled whenever they brushed close to Mike. Curious, Marina took several steps away from Mike. Gasping, she stumbled back against him. Once again, the vivid red threads recoiled.

"What happened?" he asked, holding her close to his body and looking around.

"I can see Magna's spell," she said, tilting her head.

"You can see…? You couldn't see it before?" he asked, puzzled.

"No. I can see a person's magic, but never the actual spell," she replied.

Her fingers itched to touch the threads and see if she could tell how the spell was created. For some reason, the spell was repelled by Mike. Turning, she looked at Mike. Her eyes widened when she saw a shimmering white glow surrounding him.

"What is it?" he asked in an uneasy voice.

Marina lifted her fingers to trace the glow. "I see your magic," she breathed.

Mike shook his head. "I don't have any magic," he started to protest before he looked at his arm, then lifted it to see better. He breathed out a soft curse. "What the…?"

"It's your magic," she repeated.

The vivid colors of her magic spiraled outward, touching and entwining his. Her magic changed as they combined, becoming brighter and sparkling with the same light as the stars on the water. Curious, she slowly backed away from him. She stopped when she was halfway to the water. All around her, the sparkling, soft-white glow of his magic clung to her, protecting her from Magna's spell.

She felt stronger than she ever had. Running back up to Mike, she threw her arms around his neck and held him. She didn't understand what had happened, or why this time was different, but she was grateful.

"Thank you, Mike. You have truly given me a priceless gift," she said in a voice filled with awe and joy.

~

Mike started to correct her. Relief flooded him at the sight of Marina's glowing face. She had scared the crap out of him when she collapsed earlier. Emotion choked him. Unable to voice the overwhelming feelings coursing through him, he bent his head and captured her lips. He honestly didn't care what it was or what she called it—magic, aura, a gift—he was just thankful that she was safe from the spell's horrible drain on her body.

A slight change in the cadence of the waves caught his attention and sent a flare of warning through him. Releasing Marina's lips, he instinctively turned, placing his body between Marina and the beach while his hand reached for his gun. He relaxed when he saw Orion and a group of men emerging from the sea.

Drago's dark shape suddenly appeared out of the night sky to land on the beach nearby. The relieved smile on his lips turned into a scowl when Drago's light chuckle was swept away on the breeze.

"Shit! Damn it, Drago! You are practically invisible at night," Mike snapped.

"It wouldn't do me much good if my enemies could see me coming," Drago replied with a toothy grin.

Mike shook his head. "Do you have any idea how weird it is to hear your voice coming out of a dragon's mouth? Hell, what am I saying?! The fact I'm talking to a dragon is weird enough," he retorted, running a hand through his hair.

"Nali, Koorgan, and Ashure have arrived at their designated positions on the east, west, and south sides of the kingdom. They will begin moving in shortly. If Nali and her monsters need assistance in protecting the statues, Ashure will be the closest and he has assured me that he could be here quickly," Orion stated.

Marina bit her lip. Mike could see a troubled expression in her eyes. Reaching over, he grasped her hand.

"What is it?" he prompted.

Marina looked between Orion and Drago. "King Ashure must not be allowed anywhere near the palace," she softly informed them.

"Why?" Orion asked in surprise.

Mike watched as Marina hesitated and looked out to sea. The memory of Ladonna's warning flashed through his mind—*Keeper of the Lost Souls*. Ashure must be the one who Ladonna warned them about. For some reason, Marina—and obviously Ashure—didn't want his particular talent to be public knowledge.

"You know what palaces normally have inside them. Can you image what might be left after Ashure went through it?" Mike joked.

"Gold," Orion dryly remarked.

"Jewels," Drago snickered.

Marina drew in a breath and smiled. "I'm sure my Queen and King would appreciate not awakening to an empty treasury," she reasoned.

Mike bit back a chuckle when he felt Marina squeeze his hand in thanks. A part of him felt sorry for helping ruin the Pirate King's reputation, but something told him Ashure would rather be known as a thief than a soul collector.

"We need to move. It will be near dawn by the time everyone is in place. We do not want to strike too soon. I have no doubt that Magna would use the innocent lives of your people to protect herself if given a chance," Orion said.

"I can feel the black magic. It has the same taste in the air as it did during the wars. You should have killed the bitch when you had a chance, Orion," Drago snorted, looking at the thick tangle of trees before his gaze moved up the rocky face of the cliff. "I'll save you the trouble this time," he added, looking back at Orion.

Orion grimly nodded. "I feel the dark magic as well. I have fulfilled my obligations to the laws of my people. If you want to kill her, I will not stop you, but be warned that even with her death the spell she cast over your people may not be broken," he cautioned.

The large dragon nodded his head before turning his gaze to Mike. Drago stared down at him with intense eyes that glowed with an internal fire, sending a shiver of unease through him. Mike wanted to groan when Drago bared his teeth in warning before he spoke.

"Speaking of mates, when this is over, don't try to talk my mate into returning to your world. She isn't going, even if she did threaten to if I didn't come back. Dragons don't give up their treasure, and Carly is mine," Drago informed him.

A sudden acuity struck Mike as he gazed at the huge dragon—Drago was afraid of losing the woman he loved. It dawned on him that his sudden appearance in this world had deeply shaken Drago and Orion. He couldn't believe that he was just now comprehending that they were worried that his presence might somehow jeopardize Carly and Jenny remaining here.

The thought hadn't even entered his mind—well, not for long anyway. It hadn't taken him long to see that both women were where they wanted to be. Besides, he reasoned, who in their right mind would argue with a dragon? After seeing Carly Tate in her dragon form, he wouldn't want to think of the damage she could do back home after some of the stories he had been told. He could just imagine the whole west coast going up in flames if she caught a cold!

"Like I said before, my job was just to make sure she was safe. I'm glad she is here and not dead. I can close the case, that is all I care about," Mike assured the dragon.

"Good. Orion, I'll wait for your signal above the palace," Drago replied.

Drago turned and walked several yards down the beach before he took off. "Is he always this pleasant before a battle?" Mike asked with a hesitant laugh.

"I think the better question to ask is if he is ever pleasant. Of course, he is probably scared and doesn't want to admit it. You saw his three children. Drago is probably terrified he would get stuck with them alone, especially Little Jenny-Roo. Drago told me she is a lot like her mother. Drago had to fireproof the paper birds the last time Roo was sick," Orion chuckled.

Marina smothered her laugh. "If you follow me, your Majesty, I will show you and your men the way to the river," she said with a sigh of apprehension.

Mike could feel the adrenaline kick in. It was showtime. He turned and walked back to the tree where his jacket and Mr. Bow were lying on the grass. Picking up his jacket, he slipped it on, double-checked his gun to make sure the safety was on, and picked up Mr. Bow.

"I feel normal," Mr. Bow exclaimed.

"It must be my magical mojo," Mike chuckled at the excited hum of the bow. "I just hope you feel that way when we get to the palace."

Mr. Bow quivered. "You stay near Marina and I'll fire my arrows," he promised.

"Deal. Whatever you do, make sure you protect your mistress," Mike quietly ordered.

"Always," Mr. Bow softly answered.

He returned to Marina where she was quietly talking to Orion. She reached for Mr. Bow, smiling at Mike when she felt the familiar hum of magic in the wood. He nodded in acknowledgement.

"Mike and I will find the King and do everything we can to keep him safe," Marina finished.

Orion nodded and turned to his Captain of the Guard standing silently behind him. "Kapian, just in case, have two of the men fall back and cover the rear. I do not trust Magna. She could have some of her other unnatural creatures patrolling the inner perimeter of the palace."

"Anything made of magic will be weakened," Marina said.

Orion pursed his lips and shook his head. "It is her non-magical creatures I worry about. The inky blackness that attacked me in the throne room was not made from Magna's magic. It was something else. She will keep whatever it is close to her," Orion replied in a terse tone.

"I know that the Hellhounds are not easy to destroy. I have only seen the other creature once, the day the Sea Witch changed my brother to stone," Marina responded in a solemn voice.

"We will do everything we can to stop her and restore your people, Marina. Kapian, make sure the men use full charge on their tridents," he ordered.

"Full charge, men," Kapian ordered the men standing behind them.

"Lead the way, Marina. We only have a few hours until sunrise," Orion said.

CHAPTER TWENTY-ONE

An hour later, the small group emerged along the edge of a narrow but deep ravine. The wide waterfall fed the underground river that surfaced on the other side of the palace walls and flowed into the pristine lake on the palace grounds. Marina knew from experience that the water was deep.

"Please be careful, your Majesty. Isha once told Father that he swam the underground river to see if it was possible. There are many caves that dead end. There are also eels, sharp rocks, and passages that he said he was barely able to squeeze through. Once you enter, the swift current will prevent you from coming back out this way," she warned, staring down at the glittering mist shining in the moonlight.

"You needn't worry, Marina. My men and I are very adept at handling anything under the water," Orion dryly reminded her.

She released a self-conscious snort. "I'm sorry, your Majesty. Tonight may be the only chance we have to save my people," she replied with a bow of her head.

"There is no need to apologize. We will be successful," Orion told her, touching her chin so she was forced to look at him. "I promise."

Her expression softened, and she smiled. "I believe you," she murmured.

Orion dropped his hand and nodded to Mike, who stood to the side. "Safe journeys. We will see you at the palace," he said.

"Good luck," Mike automatically responded with a nod of his head.

Marina watched as Orion nodded to Kapian before he dove off the side of the cliff into the turbulent waters below. The others quickly followed. She waited to see if they surfaced, but they didn't. She hoped they would be successful.

It would be a fight to get through the waters, even for the sea people. Once the men were inside the palace, Orion and his men must kill any of the Hellhounds that patrol the interior courtyard while one of his men opened the gate for Nali and her monsters.

Now that her magic was restored, she could seek the aid of the trees and other plants to help them. Once Nali and her monsters secured the statues in the courtyard, Orion, Drago, Marina, and Mike could enter the interior of the palace and discover where the Sea Witch was holding the King.

"Let's go," Mike said in a quiet voice.

"Yes," Marina responded with a slight nod.

They wove their way through the forest to the eerily silent outer city. She turned and headed through the park that was adjacent to the palace grounds. Running down the same path she had traversed nearly a year before, they wound their way through the forest to the outer wall of the palace.

"Please Mr. Tree, guide us safely to the other side of the wall," Marina softly requested.

She breathed a sigh when the vines hanging from the tree reached down. Lifting her arms, she waited for the vines to wrap around her wrists. Mike hesitated a moment before he reluctantly did the same.

She heard Mike's swiftly inhaled breath when the vines lifted them off their feet.

Seconds later, they were lowered to the ground on the other side of the wall. Marina blanched and stumbled back from the interior wall when she saw the tangle of black moving along the stone wall. They had escaped the creature's detection by not climbing on the wall. Marina could see the skeletal remains of birds, small mammals, and insects, which had not been so fortunate, caught in the thick tentacles.

"I don't understand," she whispered as she stared at the moving vines. "If the Sea Witch used her magic to enchant these vines, they should be normal. The spell she cast should have weakened, just as it does with the ogres. I think this isn't magic, but the same creature that chased me before."

"A creature?" he muttered, stepping back when the curling vines twisted toward him.

Marina frowned, puzzled. "Perhaps this is its natural form."

"Whatever in the hell it is, we need to stay out of its reach and get to the palace," Mike grimly pointed out.

Marina nodded and looked around them. She waved her hand to Mike to follow her. They moved through the maze, staying in the middle where the light of the moon shone. Several times, they were forced to pause when they saw a black tentacle stretching across their path.

"We will have to go a different way," she whispered.

The path leading to the main garden was blocked. The moving tentacles looked like a bed of boiling worms or snakes. Backing away, she signaled to turn left. She began to worry that they were taking too long. Turning to the right, she could see a narrow side entrance to the maze. This one came out near the sheds that housed the supplies for the gardeners.

"Marina, run," Mike hissed.

She glanced over her shoulder and gasped. Behind them, the black tentacles had transformed into thick spears that were moving through the maze. Bursting into a run, Marina focused on the opening. Behind her, she could hear Mike's steady breath, the sound of his feet hitting the ground, and the snapping of wood as the spears struck the limbs of the bushes behind them. She bit back a cry of frustration because she was unable to protect the century-old plants.

"Hang on!"

The sound of Mike's voice penetrated her mind a second before his arm wrapped around her waist, and they went flying through the air. Mike turned, holding her against him before they hit the ground and rolled.

Breathing heavily, they looked over their shoulders at the entrance to the maze. Jagged, sharp points a foot apart sealed the entrance. They would have been impaled if Mike had not grabbed her and jumped out of the maze.

"It must have sensed something was in the maze," she whispered, watching as the deadly tentacles slowly retracted.

"Yeah," Mike said, rolling onto his back and staring up at the starlit sky for a moment. Above them, he could barely make out the silhouette of Drago as the Dragon King flew across one of the bright moons. Rolling to his stomach, he pushed up off the ground and held his hand out to help Marina up. "Are you alright?"

"Yes, I think so," she replied, bending to pick up Mr. Bow off the ground before she grabbed Mike's hand. "What do we do now? How can we fight such a creature?"

Marina didn't want to admit that she was terrified. This creature the Sea Witch had under her control was far more powerful than anything she'd had to deal with so far. The Hellhounds were bad enough, but at least she knew she could kill them. This creature was different.

Mike glanced around. A slow, menacing smile curved his lips. He turned and pulled her along with him.

"Come on. I have an idea," he said, heading for one of the buildings.

~

Mike cut around the side of the building, making sure it was safe first. Peering through the window, he grunted. He could see an open door on the other side. Keeping his back to the wall, he turned the next corner. A large cart stood next to the building, a few feet from the open door. Beside it stood two men petrified in place. One held a large bag while another carried a bundle of wood under his arm. Their heads were turned back toward the palace. Their stone faces etched with expressions of confusion and fear.

"This is what she did to the entire population of dragons except for the Dragon King. In some ways, I wonder if it would have been more merciful than to live with the fear of knowing what could happen," Marina quietly said, walking up to run her fingers along one of their faces.

"As long as there is one person who can stand up to Magna and fight, there is always a chance of breaking the spell and freeing those who were imprisoned," Mike sharply retorted.

"How can we fight her and that creature?" she asked.

Mike could see the hopelessness seeping into her eyes. Stepping forward, he turned her around to face him and cupped her face. They wouldn't give up now.

"Trust me, Marina. I swear I will do everything I can to free your people. Tonight is the night. Believe in that. We have a kick-ass team with some of the scariest warriors I've ever seen in my life. If anyone can defeat Magna and that black thing, we can," Mike softly and passionately vowed.

He saw her swallow, and her look of doubt and despair dissolved into determination. She nodded, rose up on her toes, and brushed a kiss across his lips. Pulling back, she gave him a shaky smile.

"What is your plan?" she asked.

"Fire! Just about everything hates fire," Mike said with a confident grin.

"Except dragons," she said.

Mike raised an eyebrow at her and tsked. "Okay, I'll give you that. I'm willing to bet my collection of autographed baseballs that thing doesn't like it though," he said.

He watched as a glimmer of excitement lit up Marina's eyes. She bit her lip and glanced at the cart. Walking over to it, she began gathering up some materials. She searched the cart, opening several jars until she found what she was looking for.

"What are you doing?" he asked, following her.

She glanced around, her eyes darting to a pile of debris off to the side of the building. "I need several long poles," she whispered, lifting the cloth and the jar. "I can make torches."

Mike gave Marina a sharp nod. "I'll get some," he replied, turning toward the pile.

He returned and watched for a moment while Marina set the items she had collected down on the ground and straightened. Glancing around, she rummaged in the cart again, pulling out the largest clay bowl she could find. She returned to the other items on the ground.

Tearing the material into strips, she placed them to the side while she poured the contents from the jar into the bowl. She glanced up at him when he held out four poles, each one approximately three feet long. In his other hand, he held a small box that had been on the ground next to the pile.

"These should work," she said with a nod.

Mike watched as she took one of the poles and quickly wrapped the cloth around the end. She attached the strips to the remaining poles and dipped the fabric ends into the thick gel.

"Do you have any more of that gel?" he asked, placing the box on the seat of the cart.

"Yes, there are several more jars. Look for the ones with a red stripe. That shows they are flammable. What is in the box?" she asked.

"I'm going to make some Molotov Cocktails," he replied, pulling out several of the small jars and lining them up on the edge of the cart.

Mike grabbed one of the jars, pried the lid off, and carefully filled it with the thick gel. He continued to do this until he had filled three dozen jars before placing the lids back on them. Opening several crates, he discovered a stash of wax and wicks.

Reaching into his pocket, he pulled out a small knife and cut a two-inch piece of wick for each jar. He used the corkscrew on his knife to punch a hole in the top of each lid. He carefully threaded the wick through the holes. He reached back into the box and pulled out a long candle and a round metal tube that he discovered was a lighter. Flicking the top back, he aimed it at the wax on the candle. Marina watched in fascination as he sealed the top around each wick.

"What does this Molotov cocktail do?" she asked, curious.

Mike grinned. "It makes a big fire. When I was a kid, I was grounded for a month when I made one and threw it on a pile of firewood my dad had just chopped. I spent the month chopping wood to replace what I had torched. It wasn't so bad, though. My dad helped me, and I grew to appreciate how much work it took to chop that much wood," he replied with a mischievous wiggle of his eyebrows.

"Most children would have resented their father for making them work so hard," she replied with a glitter of amusement in her eyes. "Why didn't you?"

Mike held up his arm and bent it to show off his muscle. "Most kids didn't end up with huge muscles by the end of the summer," he replied with a grin. "All the girls in school were after me that year."

Marina gave him an indignant sniff and lowered her head to focus on her torches. "I can imagine they would have been anyway. I was popular with the boys in my village. None of them could handle a powerful bow the way I could," she retorted.

He softly chuckled. "I don't think it was just the bow, Marina," Mike murmured.

She looked up and raised an eyebrow in inquiry. "Why do you say that?" she asked, her breath catching at the fiery look in his eyes.

Mike leaned forward and cupped her chin in his hand. "While they may have been aware of your prowess with the bow, I believe they were definitely just as aware of the beautiful woman holding it."

"Mike, you know I love it when your voice gets deep like that," Marina breathed before her eyelids fluttered closed as he leaned in to kiss her.

Several seconds passed before he reluctantly ended the kiss. As much as he wanted to continue kissing her, now was not the place or the time. Still, he couldn't resist brushing another quick one across her lips when she released a soft sigh. She opened her eyes and gazed at him with a slightly dazed look.

"There really is magic between us. This is something special, Marina. When this is over, I want to make a life with you," he said in a guttural tone.

Marina bit her bottom lip and looked at him with a somber expression. "Even if it means you may never see your world again, or your sister?" she asked.

Mike was silent for several seconds before he leaned back and looked down. From the rigid expression on his face, she knew he was thinking about all that he would leave behind. Something deep inside told her that she could not go to his world. She didn't understand why, but it was as if something warned her that she would not be allowed to exist as she was.

"We'll discuss this more when this is over," he replied, looking back up at her. "But the answer is yes. I would leave my world behind to remain here with you."

He saw the relief sweep through her eyes. Her joy was tinged with regret. She knew that making such a decision would always haunt him.

Mike turned and finished making small, powerful fire bombs while she picked up the torches in one hand. Mr. Bow muttered under his breath that he did not like being near anything that could make fire.

"You know, I'm made of some of the richest wood on the isle. Elder trees do not burn gracefully," Mr. Bow muttered.

"You do not need to worry, Mr. Bow. If all goes well, you will be back to shooting arrows soon," Marina assured her bow.

"I can do it if Mike is near," Mr. Bow informed her.

Marina looked up at Mike with a raised eyebrow. "Is that true?" she asked.

"He said he felt normal when I held him," Mike informed her, packing the jars into a large, leather knapsack and pocketing the lighter.

"I truly hope he is. We may need his assistance," she replied.

He paused and looked at her. "Are you ready?" Mike asked.

"Yes."

Even from a distance, Mike could see the mass of black vines moving against the palace walls in the moonlight. Nodding, he motioned for her to lead the way. They would walk through the open area near the lake and work their way around to the front courtyard and gates. Looking up, Mike saw Drago begin his descent down to the lake. He took a deep breath when he saw the dark shadows of Orion and his men emerging from the water.

"Orion and Drago have arrived," Mike pointed out.

"We must meet up and warn them of the vines," she said, swerving toward a wide path leading toward the others.

CHAPTER TWENTY-TWO

The white pebbled path shone in the moonlight. As much as Marina hated the sound of their footsteps echoing in the night, she disliked the dark patches in the soft grass even more. Behind her, she could hear Mike keeping pace with her.

They reached the circular fountain at the same time that Orion and his men did. Behind the group, she could see Drago in his dragon form baring his teeth at the wisps of black tentacles.

"This looks like the evil magic that Magna has cloaked herself with," Orion said as a greeting.

"She has spread herself out too much in an effort to secure both the interior inner and outer areas of the palace," Drago observed.

"Why would she do that? Surely she realizes that it would weaken her defenses," Kapian said.

"You need to be cautious. Even as thin as these appear to be, they can be deadly," Mike warned.

Marina nodded. "We came through the maze. The black mist came together into deadly spears. It can exist in many different forms. We barely escaped," she said.

"Kapian has two men working on opening the gates for Nali. We must get inside the palace. Do we know if Koorgan and Ashure were successful in securing the villages?" Orion asked.

"Yes, I saw them come ashore. Remind me to never make Koorgan or his men mad. There were a few stray Hellhounds on the loose that didn't make it back to the palace before nightfall," Drago shared.

"What happened to them, if I may ask, your Majesty?" Kapian inquired.

Drago gave everyone a sharp-toothed grin. "Let's just say they pop when you step on them. The farmers are going to have a large area of fertilized farmland for a while."

"Gross. At least with my magic arrows they disintegrate," Marina replied with a shudder.

"I will remain by your side per my orders from Queen Jenny," Kapian stated

Orion shook his head and chuckled before he turned to Marina. She saw his expression turn to one of cold determination and knew he expected her to lead the way. Marina nodded and turned on her heel.

She gripped Mr. Bow in one hand and the torches in the other. She kept a wary look out for the black wisps. She wasn't sure how they were tied to Magna. Her biggest fear was that the Sea Witch was already aware of their presence.

They made it to the front of the palace. The walls all the way around were covered in the black vines. She was surprised that they had not encountered any of the Hellhounds so far. The thought had no sooner flashed through her mind when she saw a movement out of the corner of her eye.

"Look out!" she cried, turning as three Hellhounds emerged from between the stone captives littering the courtyard.

"Protect the statues," Orion ordered, pointing his Trident at the Hellhound in the lead.

Marina instinctively lifted Mr. Bow and uttered the magic spell she had used so many times before. The bowstring glowed faintly before fading as she tried to pull it back. She reached for it again as the second Hellhound turned toward her.

Power surged through her when she felt Mike's hand on her back. Mr. Bow hummed to life, the powerful glow of the string vibrated in her hands. Marina pulled back the string and released one magical arrow after another at the beast. The third arrow struck it through the forehead and it disintegrated into a puff of ash mere feet from her.

Marina turned on the third Hellhound. Two of Orion's men were firing bolts of electricity at the beast. Her arrow struck it in the side at the same time as the men buried their tridents into it. The beast glowed brightly before dissolving into a pool of ash.

"Orion!" Mike shouted.

Orion had sprung upward, flying over the head of a snapping Hellhound. He turned and landed on its back. Raising his trident above his head, he brought it down on the Hellhound's neck with such a force that the creature stumbled before its head was severed, and its body rolled to the side. Marina turned and fired arrows into both the body and the head.

"Look out!" Mike yelled, grabbing her around the waist and pulling her down to the ground.

Long tentacles from a black vine crawling along the palace walls struck out with deadly force. Three of Orion's men grunted and crumpled to the ground as sharp spears pierced their bodies. Drago turned and ejected a long blaze of fire on the vines, driving them back.

"There!" Marina breathed out, pointing to one of Orion's guards who was fighting against the moving vines. "We have to help him!"

"Stay back until I tell you," Mike ordered, rolling to his side and pulling one of the small jars out of the knapsack. Yanking the lighter out of his pocket, he lit one of the Molotov cocktails. "Now!" he shouted as he tossed the flaming jar at the vines.

They both rushed forward as the jar exploded, sending flames up the withering vines. The guard fell back several steps and glanced at Mike in surprise. Mike tossed two of the small jars to the guard. The man nodded in understanding. Throwing the jar toward the top of the vines, the guard aimed his trident at it and fired a bolt of electricity. The flammable liquid exploded, raining fire from the top of the vines downward.

Mike turned and threw three more jars while Marina lit two of her torches from the burning creature nearby. She gave one to Mike. They jabbed them at the twisting vines, sending the thorny limbs into retreat while Orion and his men worked at killing the half-dozen Hellhounds that had converged on the courtyard to stop them.

Marina's anguished cry echoed above the sounds of fighting and the crackle of the fire. A large Hellhound had knocked over two of the statues which shattered and turned to ash. Her fingers trembled as she pulled back on Mr. Bow. The Hellhound was heading straight for Isha. The glow of the bowstring faded when she pulled it back.

"Mike! We need Mike," Mr. Bow frantically said.

"Mike!" Marina screamed, searching for him through the smoke.

Mike turned to her. He ran toward her, but Marina knew he wouldn't make it in time. Her lips parted on a scream of denial as the Hellhound raised a sharp paw to swipe Isha out of its way. The scream died on her lips when the Hellhound was suddenly lifted in the air and tossed against the front doors of the palace.

"What the…?" Mike choked.

Marina felt him grab her around the waist and pull her to the side as a swarm of monsters swept through the courtyard. The Cyclops, Minotaurs, and Centaurs circled around the statues, forming an impenetrable wall.

"It is Nali!" Marina half-cried, half-cheered as the Empress stood protectively over her brother.

"That's Nali… and Charlie?! How in the hell did Charlie get here?" Mike whispered in shock, staring up at the monster that was the size of a giant before his gaze lowered to the pup that was excitedly barking next to Isha's statue.

Nali lifted her head and snarled. The ground trembled with the sound. Marina pulled her gaze away from Nali when Kapian came up to them.

"Hurry!" Kapian ordered, turning and firing on another Hellhound. "There are more than we thought. Nali and Ashure will handle the ones outside."

"Ashure! He shouldn't be…," Marina started to protest.

She glanced over her shoulder when Mike grabbed her left arm while Kapian held onto her right. They pulled her to the front doors of the palace that now stood wide open. Drago burned away any residual vines that had survived.

Marina pulled free and grabbed the two unlit torches. Shivering, she followed Kapian as he entered the palace. Behind her, Mike followed, then Drago. She could only hope they were in time to save the King and Queen.

Mike glanced behind them as they entered the palace. Outside, in the courtyard, flashes of light and the screams of the Hellhounds echoed through the night. He caught a glimpse of Charlie's golden body in the protective circle of Nali's monsters. With a shake of his head, he still couldn't believe the huge monster snarling out orders was the slender Empress that he had met.

Nali's appearance shocked the shit out of him. How could someone so —whatever—turn into a monster that looked like something out of a 1930's King Kong meets the Abominable Snowman movie? Well, okay, with her long white hair she looked more like a female version of an Adorable Snowwoman rather than King Kong, but still—what the hell? He wondered what other talents the amazing Empress of the Monsters had.

With a shake of his head, he forced himself to focus on their present situation. The danger was far from over. If anything, it was just beginning.

"Where do you think Magna would hold the King?" Mike asked as they stepped into the cold foyer.

"I suspect she keeps him in the throne room. As long as he remains on the throne, he keeps his power. Magna would know that if King Oray were to abdicate the throne, she would lose any chance of using the gift from the Goddess against the other kingdoms," she explained.

"What's so important about this gift? Why should it matter who has it?" Mike asked, glancing around with a frown.

Everything was icy cold, and he swore he could see something moving in the shadows. It was probably more of the black shit that made up the vines. He moved his hand to his gun holster, undid the snap, and pulled his gun free.

"Our King is a good leader. Queen Magika and King Oray protect the Orb of Eternal Light. It is what gives us our magic. Without both of them, the light will fade and so will our kingdom," Marina explained.

"I don't like the sound of that. Look out," Mike hissed, pulling Marina back as one of the shadows reached greedily for her. "What is this stuff?"

"I don't know," Marina whispered in a trembling voice. "Before Magna came I never saw anything like it."

"Be careful, I see it moving over the walls," Kapian said.

"Where's Orion? Hell, where did Drago go?" Mike asked, noticing that Drago had disappeared as well.

"Orion searches to make sure the Queen is safe. I swore to Queen Jenny that I would protect him," Kapian said, glancing at the two of them.

"Go. If you find them, let them know we are heading to the throne room," Mike said.

"Be careful," Kapian instructed.

"You, too," Mike warned, watching as Kapian nodded and turned to disappear down the long corridor. Mike swept his gaze over the shadows. "You'd better light the torches."

Marina nodded and quickly lit the last two torches. She handed one to Mike. She watched as he swung it towards the dark shadows. The creature pulled back with a loud hiss, shrinking away from the flames.

"You were right. Whatever it is, it does not like the flames," Marina whispered.

"Do you know the way to the throne room?" he asked.

"Yes, follow me," she murmured.

Mike followed Marina, careful to keep his eyes on the shadows as they moved down the long corridor. Curious, he lifted the torch. The shadows recoiled even when the flame was not close to them. It would appear it had another weakness.

"It doesn't like the light," he observed.

They continued to move quietly down the corridor, turning several times to see the dark shadows moving behind them, but staying away from the light. Mike swallowed and gripped the butt of his gun. He doubted his gun would make much of an impact on whatever was covering the walls, but it gave him a sense of comfort. Marina's soft cry of warning drew his attention forward when another shape separated from the shadows. This one didn't shrink from the light.

"A Hellhound," Marina choked, holding the torch out in front of her.

Mike raised his arm and fired just as the Hellhound released a roar and jumped. He and Marina dove to the side and rolled as the creature landed and turned. Mike fired again, knocking the creature backwards. It stumbled and shook before collapsing with a small hole in the center of its forehead.

"Shit," Mike muttered, climbing to his feet. "Are you okay?" he asked as Marina bent over to pick up their torches.

"Yes. I am glad you have your weapon. Hold these and touch me," she instructed in a trembling voice

"Me, too," Mike muttered.

He didn't add that his weapon was down to one bullet. He slid his gun into the holster and took the torches from Marina. Gripping the two torches in one hand, he picked up the pack holding the rest of the Molotov Cocktails, slid the strap onto his shoulder, and placed his left hand against her back.

Marina pulled back the bowstring and fired several arrows into the Hellhound. He watched as it glowed for a moment before turning to ash. Handing the torches back to her, he decided he'd like to keep a couple of the Molotov Cocktails jars handy just in case.

He lowered the pack and pulled two out. He reshouldered the pack and kept the two in his free hand. With one last glance at where the dead Hellhound had been, he motioned for Marina to continue moving down the corridor.

They were almost to the throne room. Hopefully, they wouldn't encounter anymore Hellhounds, but he wasn't going to bet on it. He paused behind Marina when they turned the corner.

At the end of the hall stood a set of elaborately carved doors that led into the throne room. Two Hellhounds paced back and forth in front of the doors, snarling sentinels preventing any from entering or exiting the room.

"Your weapon," Marina whispered, turning to look at him.

Mike shook his head. "I have one bullet," he said. "It might slow one of them down, but not both."

He fingered the jar in his hand. He ran his gaze over the throne room doors. It was covered with the same tangle of vines they encountered before. His gaze flickered to the two beasts pacing back and forth. Perhaps they could kill two Hellhounds and take out the thorny vines at the same time.

"Hold this," Mike ordered as he shrugged the bag off his shoulder and knelt.

Marina quickly took the two jars and his torch. "What are you going to do?" she asked, watching as he quickly opened the bag and began tying together the wicks of the half-dozen jars that were left.

Mike glanced up at Marina and smiled. "I'm going to light this place up," he informed her in a grim voice.

Returning his focus to what he was doing, Mike finished twisting the wicks together and slid them back into the bag. He stood up and nodded to Marina as he held the open bag out to her. He started counting slowly once she lit the thick cord with her torch.

Turning, he took off running toward the snarling creatures that stood frozen in front of the doors. He threw the bag at them and dove to the side, rolling as they both jumped to grab it. The moment they did, it exploded in a fiery inferno that lit up the massive corridor.

Mike slid to a stop beside a large stone planter. Rolling to his side, he stared at the two Hellhounds that were now engulfed in flames. Their loud roars echoed as they fell back against the doors. The dark, shadowy creatures on the walls writhed in agony as they were ignited in flames. One of the Hellhounds rose up on its hindquarters before falling backwards, crashing through one of the huge doors to the throne room.

"Come," Marina cried out as she raced forward.

Mike rolled to his feet. Marina covered her face as she jumped over the dead Hellhound and through the burning doorway. Mike did the same, landing on the other side and rolling before he rose back to his feet and turned to look back. The thick gel from the jars continued to burn brightly behind them. The light from the flames drove back the vines on the inside of the throne room.

He shifted on his feet and turned to look around the large room. His eyes took in the remnants of a meal on the long table. His gaze turned to Marina when she brushed a long strand of her hair back from her face. Her eyes were glued to the throne. He followed her gaze, locking on a pair of vacant eyes.

"My King," Marina whispered as she slowly started walking toward the throne. "My King, we must get you out of here," she said in a louder voice.

"I don't think so," a woman's raspy voice replied. "You see, I need him as well."

Mike watched as a very beautiful, pale-skinned woman stepped out from behind the throne. His eyes immediately moved to the weapon in the woman's hand. The long, curved blade left him in no doubt that while she might not be able to use her magic like Marina, she could still destroy the kingdom by using the knife.

Instinctively, his hand slid inside his jacket and he removed his gun. He flicked the safety off and pressed it against his side as they continued to walk forward in slow, measured steps. Mike ran his gaze over the woman. Magna's rich black hair hung in a tangled wave down to her waist. Her skin was almost translucent, and shimmered like a white pearl. Her lips were painted as black as her hair, making them stand out, but it was her eyes that held him. There was something in them; if it was anyone else, he might have thought it was desperation. Her eyes were a light green with swirls of black in them that reminded Mike of the black vines along the walls.

"Release him, Sea Witch," Marina demanded. "We are not alone. The Sea King, King Drago, and the other rulers have joined with my people to stop you."

Magna's high pitched laugh echoed throughout the room. Mike's hand tightened on his pistol when he saw her raise the knife and lightly drag it across the King's throat. She murmured something too low for him to hear before she turned to look at Marina with disdain.

"Orion is bound by the laws of his pathetic people. He is weak and unable to harm me," Magna replied with a shrug

"He might be, but I'm not," a loud voice echoed from behind them. "I already told Orion I was going to kill you, bitch. After I turn you to ash, not even the bottom dwellers of the deep will have anything to feed on," Drago snarled.

"I am bound by the laws no longer, Magna," Orion warned, stepping in behind Drago.

Magna's eyes jerked up and she released a hiss. A long spiderweb of shadowy creatures hidden in the recesses of the ceiling swirled down in a cloud, wrapping their thorny tentacles around Drago and lifting him up. Mike heard Orion shout to his men as more of the deadly vines surrounded them. He turned to stare at Magna. Her eyes were almost completely black as she focused on Drago, Orion, and his men. He shot his hand out and stopped Marina when she started forward.

"Wait," he said, staring at Magna's face.

Marina turned in surprise. "She is enchanting you. We must destroy her," she hissed in frustration

Mike glanced at Marina and shook his head. "No, it's something else," he replied in a puzzled voice.

"I won't be defeated. You will doom your people, dragon!" Magna's voice rose when Drago shifted into his dragon form to fight against the steely threads trying to rip him apart. "NO!" she screamed as if in pain when Drago released a burst of fire at the ceiling.

Mike reacted when Magna lifted the knife. He raised his hand and fired his last bullet. The bullet struck Magna in the left shoulder, causing her to spin around. The blade flew from her hand and landed several feet away. A swirling black cloud rose from where she lay, rising up toward the ceiling and reforming.

"Fire on the black cloud!" Orion ordered, lifting his trident and aiming at the massive cloud.

Mike and Marina ran up the steep stairs leading to the throne. The King, free from the threat of Magna's evil magic consuming him, fell forward gasping and shaken. Mike grabbed King Oray's left arm while Marina slid her arm around his waist and lifted him.

Together, they half carried, half dragged him down the steps. Mike lowered the man to the floor and turned back toward Magna. His gaze flickered to the mass above her.

"Don't," Marina warned, grabbing his arm. "Leave her. This is something not from our world."

Mike glanced back, torn. The training inside him wouldn't let him just leave Magna. She was vulnerable and needed help. He turned to look at the spot where Orion and his men were firing intense blasts of energy at the black swarm. He shifted on his knee to see that Drago was also breathing fire at the swirling cloud. Whatever it was, they were barely making a dent in it.

"I can't leave her," he said, grasping Marina's hand and squeezing it. "Take care of your King."

"Mike," Marina cried out, her hand slipping from his arm as she tried to stop him.

Mike sprinted up the steps and slid across the marble tile to where Magna lay. He touched her chin, turning it toward him. Her eyes fluttered open and she stared at him with surprisingly clear eyes.

"Go!" she whispered in a weak voice.

"Not without you," he said with a glance upward.

"No," she said, hissing in pain when he started to slide his arm around her. "No, I know how to… how to kill it now. Go," she said again, this time in a voice filled with determination and sorrow. "What I have to do will kill you all if you don't. Please, give me this chance to right some of the wrongs I have been forced to do."

Mike stared into Magna's intense green eyes and turned to look at Marina. She shook her head and pointed. Glancing upward, he could see the dark swarm massing together and pushing back against the assault of Orion and Drago. He looked down when he felt a slender hand on his arm.

"Go," Magna whispered in resignation. "There is no hope for me. I would be sentenced to death anyway. Let me at least have some purpose in my life."

Mike swallowed and reluctantly pulled back as Magna struggled to rise to her feet. He turned and quickly moved back down the steps as Magna began to chant. Reaching down, he lifted King Oray over his shoulder, fireman style.

"Let's go," he instructed Marina.

Marina looked at Magna. Her arms were raised, and blood coated the front of her white gown as she chanted. Her gaze was focused upward on the circling swarm above.

"What...?" Marina started to say.

Mike shook his head and reached for her arm. "She knows what she is doing," he said. "We've got to get out of here. Orion! Get your men out of here. Magna is going to kill that thing," he yelled as he hurried past the Sea King.

"Fall back," Orion ordered. "Drago, get out of here!"

The group continued to fire as they fell back through the burned doors. Drago was the last, shifting as he stepped out. Orion gripped Drago's arm when he paused.

"Think of Carly and your children, my friend," Orion quietly said, pulling on Drago's arm.

Drago grunted and turned. Breaking into a run, they retreated as fast as they could down the corridor. They were almost to the end when a brilliant flash of light exploded behind them, followed by a shockwave that knocked them forward off their feet. Mike tried to shield the man on his shoulder as he fell.

It took several long minutes before they were able to catch their breath. Mike rolled onto his back, his ears ringing as he reached out and searched beside him for Marina. He breathed a sigh of relief when he felt her small hand grip his. Turning his head, he stared at Orion. Grief and resignation glimmered in the man's eyes. Mike suspected he'd known that Magna had not been acting of her own free will until the end when she finally destroyed the creature.

"What... What happened? What have you done to my beautiful palace?" King Oray murmured in shock, staring at the destruction. "Magika is going to be furious!"

Dry laughter echoed in the corridor along with more than a few groans. Mike pushed up into a sitting position and looked around. All of the black vines were gone. There was a huge hole in the ceiling of the throne room. The first rays of daylight shone down over the two elegant chairs that sat unscathed on the raised platform.

"Oray... Where is my husband?" Magika demanded.

Mike watched as the King turned when he heard his name. The man's thin face softened and a smile curved his lips. Mike rose to his feet and helped Oray stand.

"Thank you," Oray said, his eyes glued to his wife's frantic face.

"Oh, Oray," Magika whispered, her voice filled with trembling tears. "You're back."

"Yes, my beloved. I'm so sorry," he murmured, wrapping his arms around her and holding her close. "I thought I could stop her, but it wasn't her."

"Your Majesties...," a strong voice called.

"Isha!"

Mike heard Marina's cry of happiness. He turned and watched her scramble over the debris. A young man, only a few years younger than him, met her halfway. Isha gripped her by the waist and lifted her up in the air. Marina's delighted giggles echoed through the devastated palace corridors.

"You're okay. That means…," Marina started to say.

"Woof!"

"Charlie?! How in the hell did you…?" Mike exclaimed, turning as the pup raced down the corridor, hopping over the debris as if it wasn't there. Mike opened his arms and caught the flying body with a muttered oath. "Char… Geoff?"

Mike stared in surprise when instead of a dog, he found himself holding a laughing teenage boy. Geoff grinned up at him. Mike shook his head, closed his eyes, and opened them again.

"When the ogre wasn't looking, I changed into Charlie. Ogres aren't the smartest creatures," Geoff laughed. "I've been hiding near Isha. I knew you would come. Did you see the monsters? They are everywhere!"

"Monsters? Is Empress Nali here?" Magika asked, patting at her disheveled hair.

"Yes, and King Ashure, King Koorgan, King Drago, and King Orion," Geoff answered excitedly.

"Oh, my," Magika murmured.

"Ah, Drago, you made it. I guess I won't be able to charm your lovely wife and children into moving to the Isle of the Pirates," Ashure commented, gingerly jumping from one section to another. "Hello, Magika. You look lovely as ever."

"Didn't I banish you from the palace, Pirate?" Oray growled, turning so his wife was partially behind him.

Ashure glanced around the ruins in distaste. "Only in my dreams, Oray. You look rough, old man," Ashure remarked.

"I thought you were told to stay away from the palace, Ashure," Drago growled, folding his arms across his chest.

"Ah, well, yes, but that is unnecessary now," Ashure said, glancing at Marina.

"Your Majesties, I can assure you that King Ashure was nowhere near the treasure room," Marina said, raising her eyebrow at Ashure to follow along.

"Treasure… Oh, yes, no. I fear I was much too busy to steal any treasure this time," Ashure agreed with a grin.

"Then what are you doing here?" Oray demanded.

Ashure turned his gaze to Drago. "I came to say that several of my men reported seeing dragons flying in the direction of the Isle of the Dragons," he said.

All eyes turned to Drago. For a moment, the Dragon King showed no emotion. Mike wasn't sure if the man understood what Ashure was trying to tell him—at least for a moment.

Drago's eyes darkened to a dusky, glittering gold. Pushing past everyone, they watched as he made a path for the front entry doors. He shifted before he cleared the doors. With a loud roar that rang throughout the Seven Kingdoms, he launched into the sky. In the distance, the sounds of other dragons answering their king could be heard.

"The silence is broken," Magika whispered.

"Not quite, my love, but the Dragon King's people live again," Oray replied in a tired voice.

Mike watched as Magika helped her husband through the debris. Her hand waved as they walked and the broken pieces of the palace slid back into place as if nothing had ever happened. Mike slowly closed his mouth when he felt a slender hand pushing against his jaw to close it.

"She is very powerful," Marina said with a sigh.

"You think?" Mike muttered in awe.

"Can we go find Erin and see if Mother and Father have been returned to normal?" Geoff asked, turning to look at Marina.

"Yes, of course," Marina replied, looking at Isha.

"I need to remain here and help the King and Queen restore order," Isha said.

"I know," Marina replied.

Isha smiled at his sister and brother before turning his gaze to Mike. Mike could feel the other man's confusion. It was obvious he wasn't sure which kingdom he came from.

"My name is Mike Hallbrook. It's a long story," Mike said.

"But a very good one," Marina replied, threading her arm through Mike's.

"They are mated," Mr. Bow informed Isha.

"They're what?!" Isha exclaimed in surprise.

Marina sighed. "I really don't know why Father gave me this bow," she grumbled.

Mike's soft chuckle turned into a deep, rich laugh. He wrapped his arms around Marina and swung her around. Loosening his arms, he let her slide down his body. He ignored everyone still standing in the corridor and bent his head to kiss her.

God, I love this witch, he thought as she returned his kiss with a passion that made his toes curl.

EPILOGUE

Two weeks later, Mike stood on the edge of the palace wall, looking out at the ocean. Tomorrow, he would return to his world with the help of Queen Magika. Leaning forward, he stood on the wall and gripped the edge of the opening looking out over the kingdom. While Marina knew that he had said he would return to his world, they had not discussed when. Now, he needed to figure out how to tell her.

"There you are," Marina laughed, she finished climbing the last of the stairs and came up behind him. Her face glowed with happiness. She wrapped her arms around his waist, threaded her fingers together, and rested her chin on his shoulder blade. "I wondered where you had gone. Isn't this wonderful? I still cannot believe that Queen Magika and King Quay named this The Fae Day celebration!"

Mike chuckled at her delight in finding him. He loosened her hands enough to turn around and pulled her against his body. Bending, he buried his face in the curve of her neck. They stayed like that for several long minutes before Mike raised his head so he could look down into her eyes.

"You deserve it. Without you, none of the kingdoms, especially this one, would have had anything to celebrate. I'm very proud of you, Marina," Mike said before his expression grew somber. "I have something to tell you. I wanted to wait, but… there would never be a good time."

"What is it?" Marina asked, gazing up at him.

"Queen Magika is opening a portal for me to return to my world tomorrow. I want you to come with me. It won't take long, I … I'd like for you to be there if it is possible," he suddenly said.

The smile on Marina's lips faded. She searched his face. He kept his expression calm. He didn't want her to know that he was worried that he might not be able to return.

"I knew that you wanted to return. I talked to Father and Mother about it before begging an audience with Queen Magika. They all felt it wouldn't be a problem. You understand…," she swallowed and looked up at him with shimmering eyes. "You know I cannot stay in your world, don't you? Queen Magika said…."

Mike touched her lips with his fingers. He knew what the Queen had said. She had warned him that there was no knowing what might happen if Marina went to his world. He had asked about the possibility of Marina going with him, then discarded it, then blew all of his carefully laid plans by blurting out that he wanted her to go. He did not want to jinx their trip by mentioning all the things that could go wrong. He had spent the night thinking of them.

"I just need to take care of a few things. We'll only be gone for a few hours," he said.

"I love you, Mike. Whatever happens, as long as I'm with you, we will work it out," she swore.

Mike threaded his fingers through her hair and captured her lips. He knew she was right. Queen Magika and Marina's father had both warned him that if Marina decided to return with him to his world and they stayed, she might lose her gift of magic.

There was no guarantee, but there was enough doubt that he

couldn't ask that of her. Instead, they would return to his world long enough to leave a message for his sister, Ruth, telling her that he was alright and where to find him if she wanted to come. He would also stop by the office and close the missing person's files for Carly and Jenny. He had taken a photo of them together in front of the castle with his cell phone. It was abstract enough to be difficult to pinpoint where they were, but had a date and both women with their children—fortunately, Carly's were not in the form of their dragons.

"It won't take long," he promised as he pulled back.

"I will be there, beside you, forever," she breathed. "I love you."

The look in Mike's eyes softened. "I love you, Marina. The moment you touched me, I knew I was a goner," he chuckled, staring down into her glowing eyes.

"I'm glad," she teased.

Mike listened to her light laughter as it echoed in the wind. Turning, they looked down over the festive party taking place far below. The people of the Isle of Magic, those from the Isle of the Sea Serpent, and even the reluctant Drago, along with a glowing Carly and their three children, were enjoying the King and Queen's celebration.

Mike's thoughts turned to Magna. When they had returned to the throne room after the explosion, there was no sign of her. The charred remains of the creature that had been inside her lay scattered among the ruins of the room. Mike hoped that whatever had happened to Magna, she was finally free of the parasite that had been controlling her.

"Come on," Marina said with a grin, pulling him back to the present. "Geoff and Erin want us to join them. I will teach you how to use Mr. Bow."

Mike grinned when he saw Geoff and Erin waving at them. Charlie barked and excitedly danced between the brother and sister. It would appear that Charlie had abandoned him in favor of the two children.

"You're on," he chuckled. "I've been itching to see how that thing works."

~

"Are you ready?" Queen Magika asked, standing on the throne platform early the next morning.

Mike gave a sharp nod. Next to him, Marina nervously bit her lip. Her parents and Isha stood to the side silently watching.

"Remember, you will only have until the first rays of the sunrise. If you are not back at the place where you arrived once the sun crests on the horizon, the portal will close, and I cannot open it again. You will be trapped in your world," Queen Magika warned, stepping down until she was even with them.

"We understand," Mike replied, reaching out and gripping Marina's hand.

"Marina, do you have your Grandmother's stones?" Queen Magika asked, turning to Marina.

"Father…," Marina called, turning toward her parents.

"Yes," Ariness said, stepping forward with a small sack.

"Please place them in a circle around Marina and Mike," Queen Magika instructed.

Marina's mother stepped forward to help Ariness. Once they were finished, Cornelia stepped inside the circle and hugged Marina. Mike could see the worry in her eyes.

"I promise to bring her back," he said.

Cornelia gave him an uneven smile and nodded. "I know you will," she murmured, her eyes glistening with unshed tears.

Ariness walked over, wrapped an arm around his wife's waist, and gently guided her back from the circle. Queen Magika glanced once more at Mike, and he gave her a nod. The Queen began to chant, slowly walking around the circle until each stone began to glow.

"Oh! I almost forgot," Marina said in a soft voice, turning to face him.

"What did you forget?" he asked, puzzled.

Marina lifted her arms and wound them around his neck. "To distract you," she said, capturing his lips.

Mike closed his eyes as the colors began to swirl with a dizzying speed. He wrapped his arms around Marina and held her tightly against him. Deciding the distraction was an excellent idea, he lost himself in their kiss.

~

Yachats, Oregon

"Where are we?" Marina asked, glancing around her.

Mike pushed down the churning in his stomach and took a deep breath of misty and salty air. He knew exactly where they were—on the beach in Yachats State Park, where this whole adventure had begun. Now the question was, how did he get to his house then into town. Frowning, he remembered that the rangers had a service yard not far from the point.

"We're on the beach where Charlie and I were before you opened the portal," he explained, trying to gauge which direction he needed to go in the fog. "There is a ranger's service yard about a half a mile from here. If we are lucky, we might be able to find a vehicle we can borrow."

"Is the fog always this thick?" Marina asked, turning when he began to pull her up the beach.

"Give it five minutes and it could be gone," he chuckled.

They made their way up the beach to the path. It didn't take them long to reach the parking lot. The fog began to lift as they hurried down the road. By the time they reached the service yard, it had cleared. Mike grinned when he saw the pickup truck parked outside the shed.

Since the park closed at night, the rangers were a little less prudent about locking things. They hurried over to the truck. Mike tested the driver's door. Sure enough, it opened. He stepped back and motioned for Marina to get in.

Sliding into the driver's seat, he closed the door before he checked the visor and the glove box for the keys. Frowning when he came up empty-handed, he thought for a moment before he leaned forward and felt under the seat. He closed his fingers around the metal keys. Rookies! If he was staying, he would need to have a talk with Marty.

Sliding the key into the ignition, he started the truck and backed it up. Turning the wheel, he turned on the parking lights and pulled up to the main road. If he went out the front entrance, he'd have to pass the ranger's house. Lucky for him, he knew a better way. Turning left, he turned on the lights and headed in the opposite direction toward a service road for emergency vehicles.

Within twenty minutes, they were turning onto the main highway. Mike checked the time on the radio. It was just after one in the morning. Sunrise would happen around a quarter to eight, give or take a few minutes. He'd rather be back here with plenty of time to spare. Lifting his phone, he pressed the Home button.

"Hello, Mike. How can I help you?" a soft, feminine voice asked.

"The box speaks!" Marina squeaked, speaking for the first time since they'd reached the highway.

"I'm sorry, I didn't understand what you said," his phone replied.

"Set alarm for seven a.m.," Mike instructed.

"I've set an alarm for seven a.m.," the phone replied.

Mike grinned when he set his cell phone down, and Marina immediately picked it up and began turning it over. She shook it and frowned. Reaching over, he pressed his thumb to the Home button and it lit up.

"We use cell phones here to communicate," he chuckled.

"You captured Queen Jenny and Queen Carly's images in it as well," she said.

"Yes, with the camera," he explained, reaching over and pressing the icon. "Press the small symbol on the bottom and it will look at you, then press the round button."

Marina giggled when she saw herself. Pressing the button, she grunted when she saw her photo. Lifting it up, she studied it for a moment before repeating the process more than a dozen times, looking at each one and striking different poses.

"You have just discovered a popular trend here called selfies," Mike laughed.

"I never realized I had such small breasts," she complained, pulling her shirt down to reveal her cleavage and taking a photo.

"Okay, that is enough," Mike said, grabbing the phone out of her hand and sliding it into his jacket pocket. "And your breasts are just right," he informed her in a gruff tone.

~

Three hours later, Marina walked around the small office where Mike said he worked. They had gone to his house first. He had walked through the rooms, picking up items and placing them in different colored backpacks. She had watched him select and discard items before carefully packing other things. He had given her a number of images in frames and some of his clothing that he wanted to take.

"Can you wrap these so they don't get damaged?" he had asked in a slightly rough voice.

Marina saw the lines etched around his mouth and knew that he was feeling the strain of having to decide what he could take and what he couldn't. She had nodded.

"Of course," she said, taking the stack into the living room and sitting down on the rug.

Picking up the images, she saw that they were of his family. He had told her of his parents' deaths. It was obvious that their passing still affected him. She paused on the image of him with a woman. They were so similar in appearance that they had to be related.

"That's a picture of me and Ruth last year at Yosemite. That reminds me, I need to call her," Mike said, turning and pulling his phone out as he headed back to his bedroom.

"Damn it, sis! Don't you ever answer your phone? This is Mike. I wanted to let you know that I'm okay. Listen, something incredible has happened, but I wanted to let you know that I'm safe—and happy. Oh, Charlie is with me, so don't worry about the damn dog. I've met the most incredible woman…."

As she wrapped the photos, Marina listened to Mike tell his sister what had happened to him. Her heart swelled when he told Ruth how much he loved her and that he wasn't sure if they would ever see each other again, but that he wanted her to know that he would always love her no matter where he was.

Lifting a hand, she hastily wiped a tear from her cheek when she heard Mike's footsteps as he came back down the narrow hallway. He stepped into the room, a frown on his face.

"What's wrong?" she asked.

He looked up from the file he was holding. "They have decided there is a serial killer on the loose here. They even have Charlie listed as a victim. If they aren't careful, they'll have everyone buying guns and running around like lunatics," he scowled.

"What are you going to do?" she asked, walking over to him.

"I've faxed off the info and pictures of Jenny and Carly, left a detailed note giving my immediate resignation due to a family emergency, and mailed off a letter to Ruth telling her what to do with all my assets here. There isn't much else I can do," he replied with a sigh. "I did tell them that Ross Galloway is innocent. It looks like they are trying to pin my disappearance on him as well."

"So we can leave now?" she asked.

Mike closed the file and walked over to his desk. "I have one more phone call to make," he said, leaning down to brush a kiss across her lips. "Then, we'll leave."

Marina rubbed her arms and smiled. "Good. It is cold here," she laughed.

He paused and shrugged out of his jacket. "Here," he said, wrapping the jacket around her shoulders.

"Thank you," she sighed.

"Five minutes, I promise," he said, walking around his desk and sitting down.

Opening the file again, he picked up the phone and pressed the keypad. His gaze moved to the clock on the wall. He grimaced. It was almost five in the morning here, so it was the same in California. He sat up when the phone answered on the second ring.

"Asahi Tanaka," the voice greeted.

"Agent Tanaka, this is Mike Hallbrook from the Lincoln County Police Department," Mike said.

"You aren't dead," Asahi replied.

Mike chuckled and sat back in his chair. "No, I'm not dead," he agreed, lifting a hand to run it across the back of his neck.

"Did you find the missing women?" Asahi inquired.

Mike was silent for a moment. His mind replaying everything that had happened. If Marina hadn't been standing there looking at the photos on the wall, he would have thought he'd dreamed the entire incident.

"Yeah, I found them. Carly Tate and Jenny Ackerly are safe and happy," Mike replied.

"Can you tell me where they are?" Asahi persisted.

Mike's head was shaking even as he realized that Agent Tanaka couldn't see him. "They won't be coming back," he replied with a sigh.

"And you, Detective Hallbrook. What about you?" Asahi asked in a clipped tone.

"I won't either," Mike answered.

Silence greeted his response. Mike knew Asahi was still on the other end. He could hear the sound of traffic in the background.

"Are they real?"

Mike debated on how he should answer Asahi. Did he tell the government that, yes, there are alien worlds out there, just not as far away as they thought, or did he just hang up and not say anything else? In the end, he compromised, the pen in his hand flowing over the words he had written.

"Yes," Mike replied. "Goodbye, Agent Tanaka."

The last sound that Mike heard was Asahi's breath. He hung up the receiver. He was pretty sure it would be prudent for him and Marina to make a hasty departure. If he had been in Asahi's position, he knew he'd be on the phone already.

"Time to go," Mike said, closing the file again and rising from his seat.

He walked over to the door and turned out the light. Turning to the left, he headed for the back entrance. He knew where the cameras were, but it wouldn't make a difference. By the time Asahi figured out what was going on, Mike and Marina would be long gone.

"Are we going home?" Marina asked, resting her hand on her stomach.

Mike threaded his fingers through her hand and nodded. "Yeah, we're going home," he said.

"Good. I would not want our child living in this foggy world," she said, following him out the door.

Mike had been looking up at the surveillance camera but quickly turned back to her, Marina's words echoing in his ears. She was waiting for him. The sound of the door closing behind him echoed loudly in the early morning fog, and a new sense of urgency filled him. Grabbing her hand, he pulled her down the alley.

"You could have told me this when we got back," he said, opening the door to the truck and waiting for her to slide across the seat.

"What fun would that have been? Now, your selfie will look like this," she laughed, scooting closer to him and making a funny face. "Plus, I wanted to make sure you would come back before I told you."

Mike cursed and backed out of the parking space, glad that there was no traffic behind him since he forgot to look first. Pressing on the accelerator, he mumbled for her to fasten her seat belt. The drive back to the State Park felt like it took forever.

A few minutes before seven, Mike replaced the keys under the seat of the truck and tucked the note he had written to Marty in the sun visor. This time they parked in the parking lot near the beach.

Sliding out of the truck, he turned to help Marina down. He wrapped his arms around her and held her for a moment. He never wanted to let her go.

She reached up and touched his cheek when he closed his eyes for a moment. "Are you sure you want to do this?" she quietly asked.

Mike pressed a kiss against the center of her palm. "I've never been surer of anything in my life," he said. "How are you feeling?"

"Good. The trees here are very talkative," she said, touching her forehead. "They have so much to tell."

Mike looked at her with a startled expression. "You can hear them?" he asked in surprise.

Marina nodded. "Ever since we got here. They remember you. They said you are the man with the animal that waters many trees," she chuckled.

Mike's gaze moved to the trees in wonder. Shaking his head, he gathered the backpacks from the back of the truck, picked up the box, and he nodded to her.

"Let's go home," he said, tucking the box under his arm and gripping her hand tightly in his.

Coming next:

Off the coast of Yachats, Oregon:

Gabe grabbed the net and began pulling it in. He enjoyed the peace and quiet of working offshore. The sound of the motor, the waves slapping against the hull of his boat, and the high-pitched cries of seagulls hoping for an easy meal were his companions. He preferred them above anything else.

He frowned when he felt the net shift. Afraid it might have caught on something, he looked over the side. The last thing he wanted to do was take a chance of it snagging and tearing. It was a pain in the ass to patch. Shifting, he pulled again. This time it wasn't the strange weight in it that concerned him, but the low moan.

"What the hell?" he muttered, pressing on the winch control button. "Shit!"

Gabe's eyes widened when he saw a person in the net. Moving swiftly, he finished pulling in the net and lowered it to the deck of the rocking boat. Grabbing the side, he released it from the rigging and knelt next to the still body.

"Damn it," Gabe muttered under his breath. "I don't need a dead body on my boat."

He rolled the figure over and drew in a shocked breath when he saw that it was a woman. Yanking off his gloves, he carefully brushed the long tangle of midnight hair back from the pale face. He cursed again when he touched the icy cold skin of her neck. He was trying to find the vein in her neck to see if she was still alive when he jerked back as another moan escaped her.

"Hey, lady," Gabe said in a rusty voice. "Can you hear me?"

He watched in fascination as the thick black lashes of her eyelids fluttered for a moment before she opened her eyes. He stared down into the crystal clear green depths, wondering who in the hell she was and why she was miles off the Pacific Coast in freezing water. He was just about to ask her that when she rolled to her side and threw up all over his rubber boots.

"Ah, hell," he muttered, looking down at the heaving figure.

To be continued:
The Sea Witch's Redemption
Seven Kingdoms Tale 4

Gabe Lightfoot and his best friend, Kane Field, have stood side by side through thick and thin. Brothers by circumstance, they have seen the darker side of life, and lived to remember it. When Gabe rescues a wounded woman in the waters off the coast of Oregon, they have no idea what's in store for them…

Check out the full book here:
books2read.com/The-Sea-Witchs-Redemption

Or read on to discover a new series!

Lily's Cowboys
A Second Chance Novel

Sometimes life begins after you die.

Lily reappears time after time to help families in need, only to die again once they no longer need her. In her newest life, Lily is a housekeeper for three men who desperately need love and hope, but this time her own heart is touched in a way it never has been before.

When an enemy uncovers her secret, will the Cunnings brothers be able to save the love of their lives, or is she truly destined to die?

Check out the full book here: books2read.com/Lilys-Cowboys

ADDITIONAL BOOKS

If you loved this story by me (S.E. Smith) please leave a review! You can discover additional books at: http://sesmithfl.com and http://sesmithya.com or find your favorite way to keep in touch here: https://sesmithfl.com/contact-me/ Be sure to sign up for my newsletter to hear about new releases!

Recommended Reading Order Lists:

http://sesmithfl.com/reading-list-by-events/

http://sesmithfl.com/reading-list-by-series/

The Series

Science Fiction / Romance

Dragon Lords of Valdier Series

It all started with a king who crashed on Earth, desperately hurt. He inadvertently discovered a species that would save his own.

Curizan Warrior Series

The Curizans have a secret, kept even from their closest allies, but even they are not immune to the draw of a little known species from an isolated planet called Earth.

Marastin Dow Warriors Series

The Marastin Dow are reviled and feared for their ruthlessness, but not all want to live a life of murder. Some wait for just the right time to escape....

Sarafin Warriors Series

A hilariously ridiculous human family who happen to be quite formidable... and a secret hidden on Earth. The origin of the Sarafin species is more than it seems. Those cat-shifting aliens won't know what hit them!

Dragonlings of Valdier Novellas

The Valdier, Sarafin, and Curizan Lords had children who just cannot stop getting into trouble! There is nothing as cute or funny as magical, shapeshifting kids, and nothing as heartwarming as family.

Cosmos' Gateway Series

Cosmos created a portal between his lab and the warriors of Prime. Discover new worlds, new species, and outrageous adventures as secrets are unravelled and bridges are crossed.

The Alliance Series

When Earth received its first visitors from space, the planet was thrown into a panicked chaos. The Trivators came to bring Earth into the Alliance of Star Systems, but now they must take control to prevent the humans from destroying themselves. No one was prepared for how the humans will affect the Trivators, though, starting with a family of three sisters….

Lords of Kassis Series

It began with a random abduction and a stowaway, and yet, somehow, the Kassisans knew the humans were coming long before now. The fate of more than one world hangs in the balance, and time is not always linear….

Zion Warriors Series

Time travel, epic heroics, and love beyond measure. Sci-fi adventures with heart and soul, laughter, and awe-inspiring discovery…

Paranormal / Fantasy / Romance

Magic, New Mexico Series

Within New Mexico is a small town named Magic, an… unusual *town, to say the least. With no beginning and no end, spanning genres, authors, and universes, hilarity and drama combine to keep you on the edge of your seat!*

Spirit Pass Series

There is a physical connection between two times. Follow the stories of those who travel back and forth. These westerns are as wild as they come!

Second Chance Series

Stand-alone worlds featuring a woman who remembers her own death. Fiery and mysterious, these books will steal your heart.

More Than Human Series

Long ago there was a war on Earth between shifters and humans. Humans lost, and today they know they will become extinct if something is not done....

The Fairy Tale Series

A twist on your favorite fairy tales!

A Seven Kingdoms Tale

Long ago, a strange entity came to the Seven Kingdoms to conquer and feed on their life force. It found a host, and she battled it within her body for centuries while destruction and devastation surrounded her. Our story begins when the end is near, and a portal is opened....

Epic Science Fiction / Action Adventure

Project Gliese 581G Series

An international team leave Earth to investigate a mysterious object in our solar system that was clearly made by someone, someone who isn't from Earth. Discover new worlds and conflicts in a sci-fi adventure sure to become your favorite!

New Adult / Young Adult

Breaking Free Series

A journey that will challenge everything she has ever believed about herself as danger reveals itself in sudden, heart-stopping moments.

The Dust Series

Fragments of a comet hit Earth, and Dust wakes to discover the world as he knew it is gone. It isn't the only thing that has changed, though, so has Dust...

ABOUT THE AUTHOR

S.E. Smith is an ***internationally acclaimed, New York Times* and *USA TODAY Bestselling*** author of science fiction, romance, fantasy, paranormal, and contemporary works for adults, young adults, and children. She enjoys writing a wide variety of genres that pull her readers into worlds that take them away.

Printed in Great Britain
by Amazon

59652327R00139